A JOB WITH HORSES

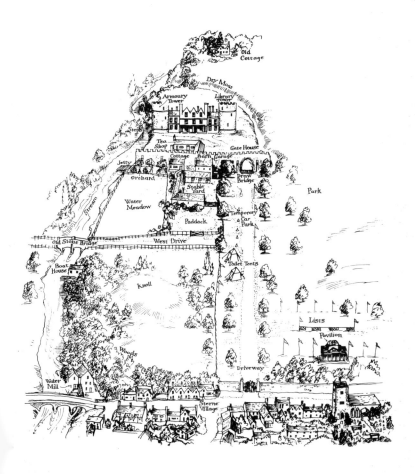

A JOB WITH HORSES

Josephine Pullein Thompson

Allen Junior
Fiction

Published in Great Britain in 1994 by
J A Allen & Co. Ltd.
1 Lower Grosvenor Place
London SW1W 0EL

© Text: Josephine Pullein-Thompson
Illustrations: J A Allen & Co Ltd.

British Library Cataloguing in Publication Data
A catalogue record for this book is available
from the British Library

ISBN 085131516 X

Jacket design by Nancy Lawrence
Jacket illustration by Jennifer Bell

ONE

I had left home and was on the train, speeding towards my first job, before my anger with my mother began to cool. As my anger faded my courage seemed to go with it, and the feeling that I was setting off on an adventure, launching myself on a brave new world, gradually gave way to doubt and dismay.

I still looked out of the train window, but I had ceased to see the spring-flushed fields and woods freewheeling past. Instead I saw Mum standing at the gate of 88 Holmwood Road and waving goodbye. Small and dark, dressed in jeans and a long red shirt, she looked great, younger and trendier than most of my friends' mothers, though her face still wore the expression, hurt but conciliatory, that had so irritated me over the last few months.

It was then I admitted to myself that, without the anger, I would never have been brave enough to have taken the job at Sterne Castle.

I was not a particularly brave or independent person. I think this was partly due to my upbringing. My father

1

had deserted my mother when I was three, leaving her to rear me on her own, and the fact that there were just the two of us had made us very close.

Of course I had gone to school and she had worked, but, though a chronic shortage of cash had forced us to live rather unexciting lives, we had always got on well and spent most of our free time together.

Greg Masters had upset everything. He had appeared around my sixteenth birthday and at first I liked him. A bit overweight, he wore glasses and some of his jokes were pathetic, but he had a car and had taken us on trips at weekends.

The fact that Mum had stopped feeling depressed, had taken to singing a lot and actually bought clothes that weren't from the Oxfam shop, should have alerted me to change, but I had been blind. It never occurred to me that their relationship was getting serious. So when on the way home from Pony Club camp she told me that they were thinking of getting married, I had reacted with shock and horror.

"But you *must* have seen we were in love, Kate. We made it so obvious," she had protested reproachfully. "I thought you realised and were happy with it. You've always liked Greg." "I thought he was just a friend. You've had other boyfriends and they didn't last," I had argued desperately "But aren't you happy for me now I've found one who *is* going to last? It's quite a hard life being a one-parent Mum, don't I deserve a break?"

Despite my desperation, I couldn't tell her the selfish truth; that to me she wasn't a person with ambitions and needs, but just my mother and I wasn't prepared to share her with anyone. Nor did I tell her that, in my eyes, she and Greg were both old; much too old to fall in love.

"I don't want a stepfather," I had answered. "I know girls at school who have them; it's a disaster."

"Don't be childish," Mum had snapped at me, "Greg is Greg, you've known him for months. You know he likes you, and you can't suddenly cast him as a wicked stepfather."

"Look, do try and face this honestly, Katey," she had begged me later, "you're almost grown-up, you aren't going to need me for much longer and I don't want to turn into one of those lonely old mums who nag their daughters to come home every weekend. If I marry Greg you'll have a proper home and you can come back whenever you like, but there won't be any need for guilt when you want to go off with friends. And that *will* happen you know; everyone grows up."

But I had always been the most important person in her life and I wasn't going to be pushed out by Greg so I had raged inwardly, sulked outwardly and was foul to them both.

Mum had done her best to placate me with special treats and extra love and when they failed, she had resorted to reason. She had seized every opportunity to point out the advantages of being a two-parent family, and launching into explanations on the difference between mother love and sexual love, with great emphasis on the fact that they were not mutually exclusive.

But everything she said or did had increased my anger, while my jealousy of Greg had made me snub his overtures, scorn his presents and sabotage his attempts at peacemaking.

Then one Saturday a couple of months later, they had

announced that they were getting married at the registry office that morning.

"No fuss, just two witnesses," Mum said, "but we would like you to come too."

It was a strange wedding. We had worn our everyday clothes and eaten a huge lunch at the local Italian restaurant with Polly, Mum's friend from work, and Greg's sister making the most of the conversation.

After Christmas we had moved into Greg's house. It was much larger and more comfortable than our flat and I was given a room with a view of the garden.

Mum had continued to fuss over me and Greg had tried to include me in all their plans, but the harder they tried the angrier I became.

I had discussed my problems endlessly with Mandy and Sara at school and they had agreed that my only hope was to get away. So when the summer term ended I didn't wait for my A level results, but announced, in the middle of a barbecued supper on Greg's paved patio, that I was going to get a job with horses and leave home.

At first Greg had merely shaken his head and talked about the importance of further education. He had nursed a faint hope that my A level grades might turn out better than forecast, and allow me to scrape into university. Mum, more realistically, had pleaded with me to take a course at the local polytechnic; for some unknown reason she favoured catering.

When my grades turned out to be almost as feeble as I had expected, Greg had begun to bring home piles of career guidance pamphlets and had even offered to pay for professional counselling.

I had refused to consider any of their suggestions. Mum apart, all the happiness of my life had been with horses. From my tenth birthday, the Croome Hill Riding School had filled the gaps when Mum was working and made up for being a latch-key child. We had afforded a weekly lesson, with extras for birthday and Christmas, and the rest of the time I had helped with mucking-out, grooming and tack-cleaning.

As I had grown older and become useful the Martins had given me free rides in exchange for my work, and later, because I was light enough to ride the small ponies, I found myself trying out the new ones and re-training those with bad habits. Since my sixteenth birthday I had been promoted to schooling the young ponies, teaching beginners and helping to escort the rides.

I loved horses, I loved riding and I was good at it. I had decided that I wasn't going to spend my life in an office or a hotel.

Finding that his calm reasoning and offers to pay for secretarial and computer courses were having no effect, Greg had finally exploded.

"Working with horses is the worst paid most menial job there is," he had shouted at me, "there's no career structure whatsoever. Silly little fools like you imagine themselves show-jumping, but it isn't like that. If you're a groom you'll stay a groom for the rest of your life."

I had shouted back, mostly about secretaries never becoming directors, but remaining secretaries for the rest of *their* lives.

Mum had tried to calm us both.

"If Kate's sure that she wants to work with horses, why don't we find out if she *can* make it into a career? Didn't

I read somewhere that you can train as an instructor? After all no qualification is every really wasted," she had told Greg, "and we can probably afford it as long as I'm working."

After that Mum and I had paid a formal visit to the Martins to discuss my future. They had been in favour of proper training, and suggested that we approached a very high-powered establishment called the Kingsdown Equestrian Centre which had just opened some seven miles from our Buckinghamshire town.

Rather unwillingly, as I was convinced that such a grand set-up would be far too expensive and anyway I wanted to make a bigger gesture and escape from home, I had written a letter asking about the courses for the BHS Assistant Instructor's exam. The answer, that they were taking working pupils as well as paying ones for the exam and would like to interview me at once, came as a surprise.

Mum was delighted when Major Braithwaite, the Principal, agreed not only to take me, but to my living at home, provided that I was at the stables by seven-thirty every morning.

Living at home had been the last thing I wanted, but Mum had discovered that she was pregnant and would only be able to subsidise me until she had to give up work, in about six months time.

I don't think Greg believed that my early rising would last for more than a week and Mum was horrified at my long hours: we worked every Saturday with only alternate Sundays off. But I decided that slavery at Kingsdown was preferable to the endless discussions about the decoration of the baby's bedroom, the arguments over the best type of carry-cot and the dithering over suitable names, which now passed for conversation at 88 Holmwood Road.

Major Braithwaite turned out to be a real monster. Short and fattish with a chunky moustache. He was fusspot, bully and slave driver rolled into one. I don't think I would have stayed the course, but for pride and Robbie's arrival, which made home unbearable. Still, we had some good times and Helen and Klaus, the two young instructors, were brilliant teachers. I am sure it was them, rather than the bullying Major who had us all sailing through our AIs with ease.

At first Mum and Greg and been full of congratulations. They had given me a huge card, a cheque for a new dress and, confronting Robbie with his first baby sitter, had taken me out for a celebration dinner at the Italian restaurant. But afterwards they had begun to talk about secretarial courses. They had convinced themselves that 'farm secretary' had a more respectable ring to it than 'girl groom'.

I didn't bother to argue, but, buying *Horse and Hound* each week, I had answered all the possible advertisements. Mum, sensing my determination, scoured the local papers, for though Greg and Robbie took up every minute of her time, she still didn't want me to leave home.

The weeks had passed and the advertisers scorned my applications. They all seemed to be looking for someone older and with experience, and I was secretly resigning myself to the torture of a secretarial course, when the reply came.

In large round handwriting, a Mrs Sterne had written

that I sounded exactly what they wanted and when would I be able to start? It seemed unbelievable.

With shaking hands I had found the right copy of 'Horse and Hound' and checked the advertisement: *Girl groom required to look after three jousting horses and children's ponies (at grass) for six months. Must be capable of taking sole charge. To share cottage with one other girl. Own room. N.S preferred. The Hon Mrs Sterne, Sterne Castle, Dorset.*

I went back to her letter. The wages weren't particularly good, but it was my first job. I would have half a cottage and I would escape from 88 Holmwood Road for the whole summer. Six months seemed like an eternity, anything could happen.

Mum had been out, pushing Robbie round the park, so I telephoned Mrs Sterne and told her I could start at once.

She had sounded surprised, but pleased, and asked if I was sure that I would be happy in the depths of the country with no nightlife. It took some time to convince her that I didn't have much nightlife in Buckinghamshire. Then she asked for references. When I had given her the Martins' telephone number she explained that, as she had no time to interview me herself, her cousin in High Wycombe would arrange a meeting. "Just to make sure that we will all get on together," she added, "though from the sound of you I'm sure you will fit in perfectly."

When Mrs Neville rang and arranged to meet me for coffee next morning, I could feel Mum listening and lurking and it was obvious that she thought an interview in The Crown meant a local job. I didn't disillusion her, but assuming an impenetrable air, commandeered the washing machine for my anorak and best jeans.

Greg had spent the evening lecturing me on the techniques of interviewers, which turned out to be rather a waste of time, as Mrs Neville only wanted to chat. We got on quite well and suddenly I found myself taking the job and agreeing to start work on the following Monday.

My elation had been short-lived and I had bussed home in a state of panic. Monday seemed so soon, and how was I going to survive sharing a cottage with an unknown girl and working for people who lived in a castle?

But then, finding Mum cooing over Rob, my anger and courage returned and I delivered my news with a sense of triumph.

I had silenced all questions by fetching Mrs Sterne's letter.

"We have three children," Mum read aloud, "All of whom ride, but they are badly in need of tuition. We are opening the castle to the public this summer and jousting is to be one of the attractions, so we have three stabled horses. However the knights do a good deal of their own grooming, exercising and tack-cleaning at the weekends and on summer evenings."

"Who are these knights?" Mum had demanded in the sort of panic-stricken voice that implied they were rapists. And, "You can't teach people to ride, Kate, not unsupervised, you've only just learned yourself. And all this bit about being in 'sole charge'; you can't have told her your age."

"Of course I've told her my age," I answered, hurt as well as angry. I've got my AI, haven't I? *And* I've taught at Croome Hill; I'm not as useless as you think."

"Oh darling, of course I don't think you're useless," Mum had wailed, as she hugged me, "but surely you could find something *local*."

But then Robbie had begun to yell, he was wet or hungry or just wanted attention, and Mum had forgotten me completely as she rushed to his rescue.

When Greg came home he remembered a television programme about jousting and seemed to be on my side.

"They were ordinary run-of-the-mill guys: hairdressers, teachers, business men, who enjoyed dressing up as knights and playing medieval war games; harmless enough," he had reassured Mum. "And what did the boss sound like?" he had asked me. "Very honourable?"

"O.K. She has a posh voice, but she kept fussing about whether I'd be happy in the depths of the country. Mrs Neville says the castle's twenty miles from Salisbury, which is the nearest large town, though it's in Wiltshire and Sterne is in Dorset. She's given me the times of the trains."

Greg had checked the time of the trains and announced that if I would catch the earlier one he would take a couple of hours off work and drive me to Reading, which would save time and the chore of dragging suitcases around London.

I accepted rather ungraciously, for, hearing Mum praise him for this brilliant idea, my jealous mind had begun to accuse him of looking forward to my departure.

My anger had helped me to remain resolute over the weekend. I had washed and ironed, polished my riding boots and managed to ignore Mum's misery.

"Six months is *such* a long time," she had wailed as she watched me trying to shut the big suitcase. "But you will come home at weekends, won't you?"

"I don't suppose so," I had answered brutally. "You don't get much time off if you're in sole charge, and the jousting will be at weekends. But you don't need me, you've got Greg and Robbie."

"Oh Katey, don't be silly," she had pleaded. "Of course I love all three of you, but you know very well that you'll always have a special place in my heart."

A pretty small place, I had thought angrily as I humped my cases downstairs.

While Greg loaded the cases Mum and I had hugged by the gate, and she had tried to extract promises from me about not staying at Sterne if I hated it and telephoning at once if I needed her.

It wasn't until the car was driving off and, looking back, I saw her, holding Robbie, and waving goodbye, that my anger tried to evaporate. But I refuelled it quickly with a reminder that 88 Holmwood Road had never been my home and that, whatever Mum said, she had abandoned me when she became Mrs Masters.

TWO

By the time the train reached Salisbury I had no anger left. I felt weak at the knees, tense everywhere else and seemed to have very little control over my possessions.

Mrs Sterne found me on the platform. "You must be Kate Winton," she said, picking up my ticket. "Here, let me take those," she added relieving me of my mac and sports bag. As we loaded my gear in to the back of a Range Rover, I saw that she was tall and dressed in a tweedy skirt and jacket, ribbed tights and laced-up shoes. Her hair was brown with a few strands of grey, her eyes blue, while her pleasant, slightly weathered face was marred by a look of chronic weariness.

Driving round the outskirts of the city, she chatted brightly, pointing out the spire of the Cathedral and complaining about the problems of parking, which was just as well for I had suddenly found myself tongue-tied with shyness.

We were soon in the country and climbing into hills that seemed older and more mysterious than the friendly Buckinghamshire Chilterns. We passed through picture

12

postcard villages of thatched cottages, and saw solitary farms sheltering in valleys or beneath hanging woods.

When my voice returned I remarked on the beauty of the countryside and Mrs Sterne smiled encouragingly and said that her cousin had told her I had never worked away from home before, so I was bound to feel a bit homesick.

Then she asked if I had brothers and sisters. I explained that I had recently acquired a stepfather and a baby brother and I suppose there was a note of bitterness in my voice, for she gave me a sharp sideways glance and said, "That can make for rather a difficult situation."

"Only for me," I answered, "the others all seem very happy."

"Then I think you were wise to come away for a few months," she told me. "I'm not sure that absence makes the heart grow fonder, but it certainly gives you a chance to stand back and find a new perspective."

Cheered that someone saw wisdom in my actions, I listened as she talked about her children: Felicity, aged twelve was a keen, but unorthodox rider, Charlie, eleven, was a clever complex character who didn't seem to know what he wanted from life yet.

"He doesn't really care about riding," Mrs Sterne explained, "and I'd let him give up if he had any other outdoor interest to put in its place, but I won't have him spending days on end shut up with a computer. I tell him he must have a number of interests; it's all too easy to let these obsessions take over. Now Ben," her face lit up, "he's nearly ten and enjoys everything; enthusiasm is a great gift.

"I'm afraid we made a mistake in giving them ponies

and letting them teach themselves," she went on
thoughtfully. "But at that time there wasn't a satisfactory
riding school anywhere near. Now we're hoping that
you will instil some orthodoxy. That's why we were so
anxious to find someone who was trained; you'll know
what you're doing and yet you're young. We did have an
older person helping out. She knows a great deal about
horses, but she's rather eccentric and the children didn't
take to her."

As Mrs Sterne described the unorthodox Felicity and
the negative Charlie my heart sank, Mum had been
right, I thought, I wasn't experienced enough to cope.
Supposing they didn't take to *me?* But when she fell
silent I thought I ought to show some enthusiasm, so I
began a rambling sentence about liking children and
having taught quite a bit at Croome Hill, which was
more geared to children than the Equestrian Centre at
which I had trained.

I am sure you'll do very well. Now this is our village,"
interrupted Mrs Sterne.

Everything was built of golden stone. The ancient
bridge over the rushing river, the water mill, the houses
and cottages, the two pubs and the church.

"That's the post office," said Mrs Sterne driving
slowly. "You can buy practically anything there. Well,
not clothes or shoes. The Doctor's surgery is round the
corner and there's another pub and some council houses
beyond it, but that's about it. No nightlife, I'm afraid. I
do hope you're not going to be bored here. And there's
the Castle," she added, turning in through some impos-
ing iron gates.

I looked up the long gravelled drive and was disappointed. I had been imagining a picture book castle with towers and turrets, moat and drawbridge. But only two towers of Sterne Castle remained and a house, in the same weathered gold stone, had been built between them. The moat, a brimming stream on the left-hand side, was dry and grassed over on the other three. A gate-house arched over a wooden bridge which crossed the dry moat, stood alone, for most of the tall battlemented walls which should have circled the castle had vanished. On this bright spring day its green lawns and drifts of daffodils looked lovely—lovely, but tame. I couldn't believe the castle had ever seen a battle in its life.

"It all looks very beautiful. Beautiful and peaceful," I said choosing my words with care.

"Yes, it was last defended in the 1650s during the Civil War," Mrs Sterne explained, as before reaching the gate-house she turned left. She parked the range rover outside a row of garages. They were modern, but built of stone and screened from the castle and the drive by clumps of chestnut trees.

"The Sternes were Royalists," she went on, "and when the King lost the war the castle was slighted—blown up by the Roundheads so that it couldn't be used again—and all the male members of the family had to flee abroad. They came back after the Restoration and built this house out of the ruins.

"Now this is your domain," she said dragging open a white five-barred gate with sagging hinges. We carried my luggage across a square cobbled yard, surrounded on three sides by stone-built and stone-tiled looseboxes. I counted eight plus a tackroom and feedstore. Five heads looked over the half doors and one, grey and Arabian, whinnied hopefully.

The yard had none of the speckless perfection of Kingsdown: the cobbles were overgrown with weeds, the white paint on the doors was peeling. All the windows were thick with cobwebs and some were overgrown with creepers, but I could see that it had known better days. My domain, I thought, feeling slightly sick, for how could I, incapable of keeping my bedroom tidy, be in charge of all this?

Mrs Sterne was looking at me anxiously. "It's rather rundown, I'm afraid. My husband's Aunt Hermione, that's Lord Sterne's sister, bred Highland ponies before her marriage and they were kept here. The original stables were within the castle wall and we've turned what was left of them into a cottage, the gift shop and the visitors' tea room."

"It's fine," I said and then, realising that she wanted reassurance, "It all looks great; very compact and convenient."

Mrs Sterne sighed with relief. "Now I'll show you your cottage. It's tiny, but I am sure that you're going to like Lisa Adams and I know she'll be glad to have you for company. She's found it rather lonely out here at night on her own.

"Did I tell you that she's cooking for us and doing these ridiculous Jacobean Banquets, which the tour organizers insist on?" she asked as I followed her past the tackroom, the feedstore and an opening, which led to a sprawling muckheap. We went through a wicket gate at the corner of the yard and a path, three flagstones long, brought us to the door of a one-storied cottage.

"It really is tiny," said Mrs Sterne in a warning voice as

she opened the door. "Four rooms and we've built on a shower and lavatory at the back."

The door led straight into a loosebox-sized kitchen. To the left was a small sitting room, heavily overcrowded with a sofa and two armchairs. "I think Lisa has chosen the bedroom with the view of the orchard and the stream. She thought you would like to be near the stables," Mrs Sterne explained apologetically as she opened the right-handed door into a loosebox-sized bedroom.

My view was of a long narrow area between the back of the tackroom, and the looseboxes on that side of the yard, and a standing section of the castle wall. It was plainly a dumping ground, with an untidy woodstack littering the dry moat. At the far end, beyond the sprawling muckheap, an old stone hay barn appeared to back on the garages where we had left the car.

I put down my case and looked around. As well as the bed there was a chest of drawers, a hanging cupboard, a table, chair and a mirror with a shelf below for make-up. The furniture looked old, secondhand rather than antique, but no worse than Kingsdown had provided for their live-in working pupils. And they had been expected to sleep two to a room.

"It's fine," I said, answering Mrs Sterne's unspoken enquiry.

"Oh good. Now I'm afraid I must rush," she went on with an anguished glance at her watch, "I've some invoices to check and a rep to see in the gift shop. But Felicity's coming over to introduce you to the ponies and she'll show you all the best rides. Meanwhile if you'd like to make yourself a cup of coffee everything's there. Lisa said to help yourself to anything you want for lunch and she'll be bringing your supper over about nine."

When I had unpacked and stowed my belongings away, I switched on the electric kettle and explored the kitchen. Finding bread and cheese in the fridge, home-made chocolate brownies in the cake tin and apples in the fruit bowl, I settled down at the kitchen table, feeling rather pleased with my achievements.

I had managed to get to Sterne without disaster, Mrs Sterne seemed well disposed towards me and half this cottage was mine for the next six months.

But after lunch this glow began to fade. I remembered Mum at breakfast, pushing a twenty pound note and a stamped addressed postcard across the table. "The card's for letting us know you've arrived safely," she'd said, "and the money's for emergencies: for catching the next train home if Mrs Sterne turns out to be a monster or you have to flee from rapacious knights. Don't be too proud to come home, Katey. Remember we all make mistakes."

I hadn't made a mistake, I told myself firmly, but that didn't stop waves of homesickness sweeping over me. I got up hastily and, deciding not to wait for Felicity, hurried out to inspect my charges.

I introduced myself to the ponies, first to a lightly-built gelding of about fourteen hands, grey, almost white with age, he had a benign eye and a wise expression, then to an unkempt brown gelding. Young and wild-eyed he looked smaller, about thirteen-two. And then to a dear little skewbald mare who wasn't tall enough to see over the half door. I was pleased to find that all three jousting horses were under sixteen hands—standing on

upturned buckets to brush out manes and reach ears is
time-consuming and undignified—and I was talking to
the dapple grey mare with the Arabian head when I
heard voices and, looking round, saw three children
climbing over the yard gate. They were all wearing
thick, dark blue guernsey sweaters, patched jeans and
gumboots. The two boys hung back leaving the girl to
come on alone.

"Are you Miss Winton?" she asked shaking hands formally.

"That's right," I answered, "and you must be Felicity
Sterne."

"And these are my brothers, Charlie and Ben," she
went on scowling at them ferociously.

The boys came forward reluctantly and as the smaller
one, the easy-going Ben, shook hands he asked, "Can
we call you Kate?"

"Yes, of course, no one calls me Miss Winton."

"Great, we thought it would be all right, but Mum
said we had to ask. And those are Mumbo, Jumbo and
Becky," he pointed to three elderly, grey muzzled dogs
sitting in a row on the far side of the gate. "Can they
come in?"

"Yes, of course," I answered again.

As I patted the dogs, who milled round me wagging
their tails, I took a closer look at the Sternes. It was obvious that Felicity and Ben were brother and sister.

They were both slim and had short, crisp, light brown
hair, bright blue eyes and lively freckled faces. Charlie
was different and definitely ugly. Shorter and squarer
than his sister, he had a pink and white skin, very pale
fair hair, pale eyelashes and eyes that blinked nervously

from behind thick-lensed spectacles.

"You're going to introduce me to the horses," I reminded them. "Your mother was busy, she didn't have time."

"That's normal, she doesn't have time for anyone but the visitors," said Charlie bitterly.

"Don't be mean," Felicity told him sharply. "The castle has to be made to pay somehow and it's not Mum's fault that Grandfather and Dad are both hopeless at business."

"Keeping up castles costs an incredible amount of money," Ben told me as we followed Felicity to the grey pony's box. "As fast as you get one bit sorted out, another bit collapses. Sterne's got death watch beetle as well as wet rot and dry rot."

"And now erosion from acid rain," Charlie reminded him gloomily.

"This is Snowy," Felicity announced proudly," he used to belong to our cousin, but now Henry's outgrown him, he's mine." She patted the grey neck lovingly. "He's good at everything except coloured jumps."

"This is Tarka," Charlie pointed at the wild-eyed brown. "He's beastly and spends all his time bolting off. I hate riding but my mother won't let me give it up."

"And this is Romany," said Felicity, opening the loosebox door so that I could have a better view of the little skewbald. "She was our first pony and she's perfect."

"She's mine now that Charlie's too big for her," added Ben hugging the pony fiercely," and she's really great."

"Her only drawback is laminitis," Felicity told me. "She has to be kept in a bare field all summer."

"Our fields are always bare, all the good grazing is given to the cows or let to farmers to raise money," Charlie was sounding bitter again. "We've got the paddock." He pointed at the flat, squarish field running alongside the yard, "and the river field beyond, but it's shut for hay."

"The knights do their jousting in the park," Ben told me. "Up there, by the pavilion." He pointed to a spectacular white building, a sort of miniature Greek temple. It was at the top of the park, where the rising ground levelled into a wide plateau and, behind it, the boundary wall was hidden by a long spinney of trees.

"The horses aren't ours," Felicity was explaining. "They belong to the knights. Rather a weird person called Delia was looking after them. She was supposed to teach us riding, but she wasn't much good at it."

"Tarka bolted off with her too," added Charlie triumphantly.

"This is Marmaduke. "Felicity introduced me to a stout black gelding. "He belongs to the senior knight, Sir Walter Melville—they all pretend to have titles when they're jousting."

"He's mega boring and Marmaduke's hobby is trampling on human toes. Delia had two black nails," Ben told me with relish.

"We don't like Mr Melville much, but he does know a lot about the history of chivalry and Dad says he's an expert on heraldry," Charlie admitted reluctantly.

"This is Fiesta," Felicity went on, refusing to be distracted from her introductions. "She belongs to Mark Chandler; he's the best of the knights."

"I like Chris best," Ben argued, "he's got more time

for us."

"Well Mark is the best-looking, the best rider and has the best horse," Felicity answered firmly. "Chris is O.K. as a person, but he's pathetic at jousting."

"Yes, he's a useless rider and really embarrassing to watch," agreed Charlie. "I wouldn't go on trying if I were him."

"Perhaps you can teach him," Felicity looked at me. "Mum keeps telling everyone that you're trained and you've passed exams; she thinks you know everything."

"Only one exam," I protested. "And I'm supposed to teach you, not the knights."

"We hate being taught, and Chris needs it more," argued Felicity. "This is Rufus."

He was one of those spindly horses, narrow-chested and ewe-necked; Major Braithwaite would have dismissed him as a bloodweed, but he had a handsome thoroughbred head and his fine coat was a rich, red chestnut.

"Now we must turn the ponies out," Felicity told me, "and we'll need your help. Charlie can't lead Tarka because he always bolts off."

There was a gate from the yard into the paddock, but apparently, with me to control Tarka, Felicity and Ben were planning a bareback ride down the main drive and along the west drive, from which there was another gate into the field.

As I led Tarka out, I could see that I was being watched intently by the three Sternes and, when Charlie opened the yard gate, the pony made his dash for freedom. If I hadn't been forewarned he would have got away from me, but as it was I pulled him up sharply. He tried again as we turned into the drive, but I was able to stop him with a rough jerk on his headcollar rope. Then his manner changed. Appearing to accept that I was boss, he stopped rolling his eyes and walked beside me with a docile air.

"Do you want to ride him if I lead you?" I suggested to Charlie.

He shook his head. "No thanks, I know Tarka, he'll try again as soon as he's lulled you into a false state of security."

We came to the field gate, but Felicity and Ben were riding on and shouting that I must see the bridge."

"It's very ancient, probably late 17th century, and about to fall down," explained Charlie walking beside me. "So cars aren't allowed to use this drive and the gate at the far end is kept locked."

The old stone bridge was rather beautiful and, on being told that it was strong enough for at least one pony, Tarka and I stood on it and looked upstream to the cottage and the castle and downstream to the water mill and the larger and more modern bridge, which carried the traffic into the village.

"That's the boathouse," said Felicity, pointing along the bank. "We're not allowed in there because the landing stages are rotten."

"Like most things at Sterne," said Charlie in his bitter voice.

"And in that hilly wood behind the boathouse are the cascades, sort of joined up waterfalls, but they don't work any more," added Ben.

"Our great-great-grandfather built them," explained Felicity. "Just for fun. They don't work now because all the pumps and pipes are rusted up, but Mum says that when the castle's sorted out, we'll restore them as another attraction for the visitors."

"*When*," said Charlie gloomily.

I resisted Felicity's suggestion that we should go on to the end of the west drive, reminding her that I had evening stables to do. So we went back to the field and turned the ponies out. When we'd fed them with arm-fuls of sweet-smelling meadow hay, which was appar-ently home grown, the Sternes announced it was nearly their tea-time.

"We'll come tomorrow morning, at about ten, and show you one of the rides," announced Felicity in her patronising voice. "I hope you sleep well and don't start seeing ghosts like Lisa." They all three ran off laughing, before I had a chance to ask what form Lisa's ghosts had taken. But, as I changed into my oldest jeans and sweater, I decided that the cottage was a most unhaunted place and that, anyway, I didn't believe in ghosts.

Searching for the mucking-out tools, which had either been abandoned on the muckheap or were scat-tered round the yard, I imagined Major Braithwaite's countenance turning purple. At Kingsdown muckheaps were squared to perfection twice a day and tools were kept in orderly rows. The Sterne wheelbarrow wouldn't have passed muster either. It was a heavy old-fashioned wooden affair, and the stable broom was positively bald.

By the time I had mucked out and given all three horses a quick groom, I was beginning to feel weary, and the discovery of a tackroom full of uncleaned tack and a chaotic feedstore, lowered my spirits. The tack could wait, but my charges had to be fed so I explored a row of musty rat-holed, wooden cornbins, and found that they had been abandoned, but there were crushed oats in a dustbin and a sack of a chaff. On the sack was pinned a note, written in a large childish handwriting and signed *Delia*. It listed what each horse was having by scoop. As I mixed the feeds, I though of Major Braithwaite's fury at the use of such an unscientific measurement; at Kingsdown even the haynets had been weighed on a spring balance, and I wondered at the simplicity of the diet— no linseed cake, no mineral-enriched horse nuts, no boiled food, just crushed oats and chaff. Still Marmaduke and Fiesta obviously thrived on it, I told myself, and bloodweeds always look herring-gutted.

I had looked forward to tea in the cottage but the moment I sat down waves of homesickness and depression began to sweep over me. The sprawling muckheap, dirty tack and weed-ridden yard all weighed upon me, but, given time, I was capable of sorting them out. But the Sternes were a far greater problem. Felicity was ominously self-confident. I could see her challenging my authority and, if she won, turning into a human Tarka and despising me as she had Delia.

And what on earth was I to do about Charlie? And then there were the knights. . .

I felt better when I had revived myself with tea and several more chocolate brownies. I took a shower and changed into clean sweater and jeans and, afterwards, feeling that I must keep busy at all costs, I explored the cottage.

Lisa's room *was* much nicer than mine. Apart from the view of a narrow orchard in which one tree—it looked like a pear—was already dazzling with white blossom, she had managed to give it character. A Mexican-looking rug beside the bed, a colourful patchwork quilt thrown over the bed, photographs of her friends and family and two prints by modern artists which, unlike the pictures in my room, were obviously not cast-outs from the castle. All I had brought from home was one battered snapshot of Mum, pre-Greg, and a few of my favourite china animals. I began to feel inadequate, unsophisticated and convinced that Lisa would despise me.

Still, she was untidy, I thought gratefully, looking from the collapsed pile of cookery books in one corner to the heap of discarded clothes spilling from a chair in the other. And, though she had bagged the best bedroom, I found that she had divided everything else with meticulous fairness: half the towel rail, half the shelf in the shower room and two of the four hooks on the back of the front door had been left empty for me.

The television was only a black-and-white portable, but with it for company, more tea, and another raid on the tin of chocolate brownies, I managed to survive until five minutes past nine, when the door opened and my cottage sharer appeared. We met in the kitchen.

"Lisa Adams," she said, putting down a thermal bag and holding out her hand.

"I'm Kate," I answered, noticing that she was small, certainly no taller than my five-feet-three, and very slim. She had small features and brown eyes, set in a heart-shaped face that was entirely dominated by a pair of enormous glasses. Her hair like mine was dark, but long and straight and tied back. Mine, being tiresomely curly, has to be cut short in a head-hugging style to keep it under control.

"Do you like the cottage?" Lisa asked eagerly, while

her intelligent eyes scanned me searchingly through the enormous glasses. "Is your room bearable? I'm afraid I bagged the best one, but I thought you ought to be in earshot of the stables."

"Yes it's fine," I answered, "and I'll improve the view by tidying up the muckheap. Look, I was starving and I'm afraid I've eaten half your tin of chocolate brownies."

"Oh don't worry, they were really Sterne property. Whenever I make anything for them I do a bit extra for us. Mrs S. says she's happy with that so long as it's just us and we don't start entertaining hordes of friends or relations.

"I'm sorry we have to eat so late," she went on as she unpacked plastic boxes, "but I have to feed them first. I don't wash up though, Mrs White and/or her daughters do that. Would you lay the table, while I put this in the oven? The menu is cream of onion soup, wild rabbit *en croute* and chocolate mousse. Does that suit Madame?"

"Perfectly," I answered, "I was expecting scrambled eggs or baked beans."

It was a delicious dinner. I had always thought Mum quite a decent cook—her best things were pasta, Sunday lunch and homemade ice cream—but I realised at once that Lisa was in a different league.

"Just a simple meal," she insisted, waving my compliments away, "but I do admit that cooking in the castle is a challenge. All the equipment is positively antique, the poor Sternes live in a time warp—they've modernized the best bedrooms and put in bathrooms for the visitors—but the money ran out before they got to their own part of the house. Lack of cash makes the cooking complicated too. I can use vast quantities of anything

reared or grown on the estate, but hardly anything that
has to be bought."

"I need a new stable broom urgently," I told her.

Lisa laughed. "You'll be lucky."

After we'd eaten we sat talking for a long time. Lisa
said that we must exchange histories and launched into
hers. She was the second of four sisters in what sounded
like a very devoted family. Brought up in Somerset, she
had been interested in cooking for as long as she could
remember. She had acquired several diplomas, worked in
hotels in London and France and fallen in love twice.

Finding Lisa so open and willing to talk, I asked about
her boyfriends.

"The first one decided that he was gay and the second
is an ambitious type, who thinks marriage before thirty
would wreck his career. I couldn't see myself hanging
around for six years, so I walked out on him," she confided. "But then London seemed to have lost its attraction and I found myself longing for the West Country.
Six months in Dorset sounded just the thing, but I suppose I'll be longing for London by the autumn and then,
who knows, Jerry and I might get together again. Now,
what about you?"

Unlike most good talkers, Lisa was also a good listener
and she seemed determined to drag the facts of my life
out of me. So I explained that I couldn't remember my
father and told her about my close relationship with
Mum, until Greg and then Robbie had arrived on the
scene and forced me to leave home.

"I can see it's been tough," she said, when I fell silent,
"but you'll bless Greg later. I mean it was obvious that
either you or your mother would break things up even-

tually and now if you want to go abroad, live with someone, or get married, you won't feel guilty. You're free to
do your own thing without worrying about *her* being
lonely."

"Yes, you may be right," I agreed, without much con-
viction, for I knew that, feeling betrayed, I actually
wanted to punish Mum; I *wanted* her to be lonely.
Changing the subject, I asked about the Sternes.

I don't know much about the children, we try to keep
them and their awful old dogs out of the kitchen," Lisa
answered, "but Mrs S. is a sweetie. The problem is that
the place simply eats money and, as the men seem to
have been born without business sense, she's fighting a
lone battle against bankruptcy. I'm not sure if Lord
Sterne is really potty or merely eccentric. He seems to
devote his entire life to his coin collection, which is
housed in the Armoury Tower. He's nothing to look at,
square with pale eyelashes and desperately short-sighted
like poor Charlie. Still, to give him his due, he's a world
famous numismatist, and archaeologists and curators of
museums are always turning up to consult him about
some ancient coin."

"And Mr S. is no use at running things?" I asked.

"No, he wanders about looking like a country gentle-
man with a shotgun under his arm, but I don't think he
ever fires it," laughed Lisa, handing me a washing-up
mop and starting to pile our plates.

As I washed up at the tiny sink, she announced that we
must discuss our joint arrangements.

"Look, if I produce the dinner will you lay the table
and warm the plates beforehand and wash up afterwards?"

"Yes, of course," I answered, "but does that mean we're going to have a dinner like this every night?"

"Yes, except on my day off which is usually Monday, but we won't starve, I'll make sure there's something in the fridge.

Now, breakfast. Can you organize the food for both of us? I only want coffee, toast, butter and marmalade, but obviously we'll need teabags and whatever you eat for lunch. You can get it all at the village post office. Don't buy milk or eggs, they appear free from home farm."

"It all sounds great," I told her, "Especially the dinners."

"You can grow tired of rich food," warned Lisa. "You'll probably be sick of the sight of game pie, *coq au vin* and syllabub by the end of the summer. Now I must lock up. And I advise you to sleep with your window shut in case of prowlers."

"Prowlers," I repeated, "Here, in the depths of the country?"

"Yes, I know that Mrs S. and the Whites think I'm being neurotic and I admit that it *has* been a bit creepy sleeping here on my own, but I'm still absolutely positive there were people about."

"The children said you'd seen a ghost."

"No, I didn't *see* anything, but I heard real flesh-and-blood voices. I might have been dreaming when I heard voices in the orchard, but I was wide awake when they passed the cottage and I heard their footsteps on the path and the gate being open and shut."

"When was this?" I asked.

"Last Sunday at half-past-two in the morning."

"And we've no telephone?" I asked, looking round.

"No, and though the Whites' cottage is close—we're practically back to back—it's built against the remains of the castle wall and has no windows or doors on this side. And as the castle walls are a good two and a half metres thick, no one would hear anything."

"Why should anyone prowl in our orchard?" I asked.

"It runs down to the stream, so I guessed that they were stealing fish," Lisa explained. "But apparently there's nothing worth stealing in the Wendle—no trout or salmon."

"Did the Sternes tell the police?" I asked.

"No, Mrs S. made soothing noises and said it was probably the the horses. But look, you mustn't worry, it's highly unlikely they'll prowl again and, provided we lock up and keep our windows shut, we can't come to much harm. And if it *was* my imagination, I'll be fine now you're here."

THREE

I slept well, being too tired to worry about prowlers, and only wakened when Lisa's indignant face appeared round my door demanding that I switched off my alarm clock. Then I lay longing for the familiar sounds of home— even Robbie's yells for his morning feed would have been welcome, but rapturous birdsong and soothing pigeon coo reminded me, all too clearly, that this was no dream; my rash act was real and I was in 'sole charge' at Sterne. Gradually the bright sunlight piercing the unlined curtains and the remembrance that I no longer had to cycle eight miles to work, induced more positive thoughts and I struggled up, resolving to do all the mucking out before breakfast.

Lisa was sitting at the kitchen table, hugging a mug of coffee to herself and one look warned me against conversation. I made tea in silence and took my mug out to the yard. A synchronized neigh greeted me. I collected water buckets and drank my tea as I waited for them to fill from the dawdling tap.

At Kingsdown the working pupils had only done two

32

horses each, and three was somehow harder work than I had expected. This, combined with Marmaduke trampling on my left foot and the discovery that Fiesta was filthy and would need washing, made me feel that my new life was rather too demanding, and there was no Major Braithwaite to use as a scapegoat or fellow working pupils to sympathise.

Ben and Felicity arrived while I was having breakfast.

"Charlie can't ride, he's got stomach pains. Dad says they're psychosomatic, but Mum's letting him stay in bed," announced Felicity. "We need you to catch Tarka."

"I won't be long, I'm just finishing breakfast," I told her.

"Could you do a bit of tack-cleaning while you're waiting?"

"We hate tack-cleaning," objected Felicity.

"It's mega boring," argued Ben.

"But the ponies' tack is revolting," I told them. "It doesn't look as though it's been cleaned for months. You might at least wash the bits; how would you like dirty bits, encrusted with old food, stuffed in your mouths day after day?"

"We're people not ponies," Felicity answered over her shoulder as they retreated to the yard.

As I ate an apple and drank my second cup of coffee I told myself that I mustn't antagonise my pupils on the first day. I would have to introduce a new regime gradually and tactfully. But, when I went out to the yard I saw that they had washed the bits and now they were sitting on the gate, dangling headcollars and waiting patiently.

Later, when I had washed Fiesta and the Sternes had brushed the worst of the mud off their ponies, we set out for a ride with Felicity very much in charge.

We crossed the drive and entered the park through a plain iron gate, which matched the railings that fenced both sides of the drive. Though there were huge ancient-looking oaks scattered over a wide area of grassland, the park had obviously ceased to be used solely for pleasure. Electric fences criss-crossed it fencing off great squares and, instead of graceful deer, black and white dairy cattle grazed greedily and the air was sickly with the smell of silage.

"That's the tilt, where the knights joust—that flat bit with the fence in front of the pavilion," said Ben pointing.

"It's a very dramatic background, but the pavilion doesn't look quite the right period for knights." I observed.

"Well it has to do. It was one of great-great-grandfather's follies—he wasted an awful lot of money," explained Felicity in severe tones.

As we rode I took stock of my pupils and was appalled. Even Mrs Sterne's warnings had not prepared me for this. They sat in the backs of their saddles with their legs stuck forward and their hands in the air and let their good-natured ponies carry them along. When they wanted to go faster their legs waved like windmills and their heels drummed on the ponies' sides, when they decided to turn or stop, they heaved on the reins like sailors hauling boats. And the worst of it was that they seemed quite happy and at home.

I consoled myself with the knowledge that Fiesta was going beautifully. She was lively and obviously extremely well-schooled. I wondered if this was the work of her knight, Mark Chandler, or whether he had bought her ready-trained. Her only fault seemed to be shying: anything remotely unexpected or unusual, was an excuse for a leap in the air, or a pirouette, followed by flight. After the first shy at a flapping plastic sheet had nearly unseated me, I realised that she wasn't the sort of horse on which you relaxed or dreamed, and when she tried again, I was ready.

"Do you like riding Fiesta?" Felicity enquired kindly when a canter had brought us to a gate at the far end of the park and I thought I detected a faint air of disappointment when I answered that she was one of the nicest horses I had ever ridden.

"Delia didn't like her much, she would only take her round the drives and along the road. When she came with us she always chose Marmaduke."

"Perhaps I'll like him even better," I suggested, not wishing to be drawn into discussing Delia.

Out of the park, we turned left and rode through a plantation of young trees, across farmland and then along a leafy track beneath a hanging wood, until we came to a solitary hill circled by deep ditches and topped with earthworks.

"This is the Roman fort," Felicity told me proudly. "Other people have used it as a fort since, but it was originally Roman."

We crossed a shallow brook and then, as we climbed up a chalk track to the fort, I decided that as Felicity was riding beside me and I had been hired to 'instil orthodoxy' I had better begin.

"Do you know that you should keep your lower leg back?" I asked. "The rider's toe should always be just

behind a vertical line drawn from the front of her knee
to the ground. Like that," I pointed at my own leg.

"Why?" asked Felicity.

"Because in that position you have full control of the
pony's hindquarters, you can produce impulsion and put
him on the bit. And you have lateral control too, you can
manoeuvre him away from traffic and other horses, open
gates easily; it's the key to everything."

"I can do all that with my legs forward," argued Felicity.

"No you can't, I've been watching you. You can't give
correct aids with your legs in that position, so you kick;
no good rider *ever* kicks."

"Who cares about being good?" asked Felicity and,
with tremendous flapping and kicking she urged Snowy
into a canter.

"Your pony does," I shouted after her. "Ponies hate
being kicked."

"What's going on?" asked Ben appearing beside me.

"I was telling Felicity that you both ride with your
legs too far forward." I pointed. "Put them back. When
you look down you shouldn't be able to see your toe; it
mustn't be in front of your knee."

"Why not?" asked Ben.

I decided on a simplified version. "Because when you
stick your legs forward your stirrups push you back in
the saddle and then you're behind the movement of the
pony, you don't go with him."

"I feel O.K.," argued Ben.

"You'll never be a good rider then, it's impossible to
show-jump or ride across country in that position."

"Who cares?" said Ben and turned into a whirlwind of

waving arms and legs as he set off in pursuit of his sister. I followed them up a grassy slope and through a hunting gate, which brought us to the centre of the fort. A breeze was blowing and the views were wonderful. Fiesta gazed about her, obviously enjoying them too. "The sea's over there," said Ben pointing vaguely. "We always canter across the top," Felicity told me. "Well provided no one's riding Tarka—it's his favourite bolting off place."

Deciding that I would concentrate on changing their seats before attempting other improvements, I repressed a desire to tell her that always cantering in the same places was bound to inculcate bad habits, and followed them over the short rabbit cropped turf to another gate. As we slid down a slippery path I blessed the fact that they were riding such sensible ponies, for, with their ghastly backward seats they had no control and Ben left his reins dangling in loops while he took a firm hold of the pommel.

When we reached the lane below, we could hear a low humming noise and Fiesta immediately began to prance and prepare for flight. I looked over a straggling hedge and told her, "Don't be silly, it's only a metal detector."

"It's Mr Melville," Felicity sounded excited. "We've caught him in the act."

"The chief knight?" I asked, thinking that the short, stocky figure with tufts of white hair showing on either side of his tweedy hat didn't look right for the part.

"Yes, and he *is* looking for our treasure," said Ben, lowering his voice in mid-sentence. They stood in their stirrups to watch as Mr Melville walked up and down a small area of rough ground, kicking its carpet of ivy aside.

"Why there?" I asked.

"It's the ruins of a cottage, Keeper's Cottage," Felicity answered. "When it burned down Great-Grandfather rebuilt it in a better place. Come on, Ben, let's ask him what he's up to."

"Yes, I hope he turns pale or gives a guilty start," agreed Ben, riding forward with enthusiasm.

But Mr Melville was too intent on his search to see us and the humming of the metal detector evidently drowned the Sternes' shouts, so they found a gap in the hedge and rode into what had once been the cottage garden. Fiesta was still prancing about, doing her imitation of a frightened horse, but she followed the ponies.

"Good morning, Mr Melville," shouted Felicity. Seeing her he switched off the machine. "Are you looking for treasure?"

"No, no. Nothing as dramatic as that. This is my new toy," he patted the metal detector, "and I thought I might find a few old coins for your grandfather's collection."

"But you know about out treasure," persisted Felicity, "the chest of treasure that was buried in the Civil War?"

"Yes, I have heard the story, but it is only hearsay, you know, I haven't been able to find a scrap of documentary evidence and your aunt, the one who made a study of Sterne history, insists that it's all nonsense."

"Oh, this is Kate Winton who's come to look after the horses," said Felicity, changing the subject.

I tried to move nearer, but Fiesta, who was still gazing at the metal detector with bulging eyes, refused to approach, so Mr Melville and I waved at each other.

"I am sure he *is* searching for it," said Ben as soon as we were back in the lane. "He wouldn't look for coins in Keeper's Cottage, would he? I mean gamekeepers never had much money, if he was really after coins surely he'd go up to the fort?"

"Tell me about this treasure." I said.

"It's a chest full of gold and silver," Ben answered,

"It happened in the Civil War," Felicity explained. "The Lady Sterne who was defending the castle, realised that the Roundhead army was coming and that she wouldn't be able to hold out for long. So she packed all the valuables that were left, gold coins, silver candlesticks and dishes, into a stout chest, and sent some trusty servants to bury it outside the castle walls. The trusty servants were both killed in the fighting and Lady Sterne died of plague, so when, after the Restoration, her son was allowed home, no one could find the treasure."

"Dad and the aunts do think it's all nonsense. They say that every penny was spent on uniforms and muskets for the King's army, but *we* think there's a chance it's true," added Ben.

"And how does Mr Melville know about it?" I asked.

"He asked permission to study the archives in our library," Felicity answered. "He said he wanted more information on the Castle and the Sternes because he's writing this introduction for the jousting programme, but Charlie says he's always up there, and that he's stopped reading about knights and is going through the Civil War papers."

"But even if he found the treasure he couldn't keep it," I pointed out. "It would still belong to your grandfather."

"You can't be certain. Finders definitely get a share and we think he'd be sure to know a loophole in the law; he's a solicitor, you see. Well, half-retired."

"Yes, and the trouble is that Dad and Grandfather are very easy to outwit," agreed Ben with a sigh.

The lane brought us to our stream, the Wendle.

"We can ford it here," said Felicity.

"Are you sure?" I asked doubtfully. The bank was shelving and gravelled and the lane continued on the far side, but the stream looked deep and fast-flowing. "I don't want Romany swept away and drowned."

"It's too deep in the winter, but it should be O.K. now," answered Ben, "but I'll let Snowy go first to make sure."

Snowy crossed carefully and I followed with Fiesta prancing through the water at an elevated trot, which produced enormous quantities of splash and soaked us all. Romany was almost swimming at one point, but she seemed quite confident and Ben sat with his feet along her neck to keep them out of the water.

On the far bank we cantered, passing the castle and the cottage, until we came to the west drive bridge and then we walked. I decided to have another go at Ben's legs.

"Romany's a lovely pony," I told him, "but you ride with an old-fashioned hunting seat; you're a horrible sight. Do put your legs back. Go on, look down, your toe shouldn't be in front of your knee."

Ben looked down. "But that's where my feet like to be," he objected. "You're as fussy as Delia. Riding's no fun if you have to spend the whole time watching your toes."

"It's more fun if you ride properly," I argued, "You can do more exciting things like jumping and cross-country, and you can manage difficult ponies like Tarka as well as obliging ones like Romany and Snowy."

Kicking Romany into a trot he caught up with his sister, "Kate says if we put our legs back we can ride Tarka," he shrieked gleefully, "so don't put them back whatever you do."

When I reached the stables I ignored my unwilling pupils and tacked up Marmaduke. His saddle looked hideously uncomfortable: it was wide-cantled, straight cut, and covered in military-looking buckles and Ds, so I decided to borrow Fiesta's. Then, since I hadn't time to get lost, I decided to go the same ride again.

Marmaduke wasn't my sort of horse. Too solid, with straight shoulders and rather a lot of knee action, he pounded where Fiesta had flown. But he was a willing and easy ride and, without my reluctant pupils, I was able to spend more time admiring the gorgeous countryside. I kept thinking of the cross-country courses one could build: downhill jumps from the fort. tree trunks on the edge of the ford, hedges on the farmland, hayracks and an Irish bank in the park. It all seemed so wasted on the Sterne children. When I thought of the people I knew who longed to have ponies or horses of their own and would have given almost anything to have somewhere like this to ride, it seemed a dreadfully irony that Charlie had pyschosomatic pains when confronted with a pony and the other two were content to ride as badly as the lowest order of pony trekker.

On my second return to the stables, I was rather relieved to find that the children had vanished and I treated myself to a coffee and chocolate brownie break, before setting off for the shop.

The post office people seemed very friendly and said they hoped I liked working at the castle, but housekeeping proved extraordinarily expensive and I felt a stab of regret for 88 Holmwood Road, where the staple foods, stored in the freezer or on cupboard shelves, were free and waiting to be eaten.

At a distance and with no one to make me jealous, I was finding it difficult to keep up my anger against Mum and the realization that the ready stamped addressed postcard she had given me lay forgotten at the cottage, filled me with guilt.

I wrote it over lunch. 'Arrived safely' was easy, but I was too proud to add 'Uncooperative children, muck-heap a mess, broom useless, weeds everywhere. Home-sick.' which was what I thought and felt. In the end I managed, 'Wonderful countryside, dear little cottage. Lisa—the sharer—nice and v.gd cook. Horses and ponies great. Love to all, Kate.'

This was equally true, I thought, I was simply looking at the other side of the coin.

I took the card to the post on Rufus, and then rode on through the village, hoping to find a gate into the Sterne fields somewhere near the bridge. There was one, on the boathouse bank. A notice said *Private Mill only*, but I decided that it didn't apply to me. Luckily the mill wasn't working. The wheel and machinery were at rest and the pool was mirror calm, so Rufus only objected to the hollow sound his hoofs made on the plank bridge over the mill stream. At the walk he was quite a pleasant ride, but as soon as we trotted I realized that he was terrified of any contact with his mouth and a stargazer. We passed the boathouse, crossed the west drive bridge and rode along the other bank. I was planning to try the fort ride back to front, but the stargazing Rufus was no fun to ride. He was wearing a jointed snaffle, which obviously wasn't the best bit for him, and a standing martingale, which might have helped if he had flung up his head occasionally, but was no use in getting him to accept the bit. Hating his stiff back and jerky paces and the red chestnut ears that were almost in my face, I soon turned back. I would change his bit and school him in the paddock, I decided, but it was going to be difficult. I had never coped with one as bad as this before. I began to hope against hope that his knight knew how to ride him.

My last ride of the day was Tarka and, remembering the children's warnings, I took him into the paddock and shut the gate before I mounted. The far corner by the west drive fence looked the flattest part of the field so I rode across and, planning to mark out a school next day, I began to ride round. I was relieved to find that Tarka was naturally well-balanced and not a stargazer. In fact he was rather a nice ride, and I was settling down to enjoy myself when he staged a rebellion. Setting his jaw and stiffening his neck, he charged towards the stables. Taken by surprise, I failed to stop him until we were almost at the gate and then only by hauling him round in an unhorsemanlike manner. Cross, and glad that there were no Sternes watching. I took him back to the school at a brisk trot, and, using my legs like mad I made him circle very energetically as a punishment. It wasn't long before he tried again, but having learned what to expect, I could stop him much sooner. Gradually I found that if

I felt a charge coming, I could prevent him stiffening his jaw by judicious use of the inside leg and rein and he found that, without a stiffened jaw, he couldn't snatch control. After about twenty minutes of subtle battle, Tarka decided to accept defeat and suddenly became cooperative. I taught him the turn on the forehand, which was another way of getting him to flex his neck and jaw, and then trotted circles and serpentines. I was pleased with him and decided that he was my second favourite ride. He wasn't in the same class as Fiesta, but he had more potential than Marmaduke and his 'bolting off' seemed to be a bad habit, a method of getting his own way with a weak rider; he wasn't a real runaway. But later, when I asked him to canter, he shot off again and galloped flat out for the gate. I could see now why the Sternes were afraid of him, but furious at this attempt by a thirteen-two pony to bully me, I hauled him round sharply, rode him back to the school and kept him trotting circles until he felt really tired. When I cantered again I was ready for him, but this time he did seem to have accepted defeat.

There were a number of poles and oil drums lying about the paddock and I couldn't resist building a couple of small jumps. I began by trotting at them and was ready when Tarka, on landing, tried to make his dash. Then I rode him on a circle until I felt him agree to behave, before jumping again. He jumped big, but seemed full of confidence and was obviously enjoying himself and this time there was no dash to the gate. As I patted him there was a shout of "Shall we make them higher?" and looking across I saw three Sternes watching from the yard.

"No thanks," I answered riding over to them. "He's

done enough for today. Tomorrow I'll build him a little course. He's been trying his bolting-off tricks on me, but I do like him, he's a really nice ride."

"You're welcome to him," said Charlie gloomily. And Ben added, "We think he's the yukkiest pony in the world."

"We've brought a message for you from Mr Melville," announced Felicity. "He rang Dad. There's a jousting practice tomorrow evening, so you don't have to exercise the horses and you mustn't give them their evening feeds on any account."

"Great," I said, thinking that I would now be able to groom all three horses really well. I looked at Felicity. "What about riding in the school tomorrow morning then?" I suggested. "I shall have time to mark it out and organize some jumps."

"No *thank* you," she answered.

"But you'll never improve if you only hack." I tried not to sound hurt or despondent. "You have lovely ponies and perfect riding country. Doesn't that make you want to ride well?"

"No, we can stick on and control the ponies and that's all that matters. We don't want to be the sort of people who sit perfectly and wear black coats."

"All lessons are mega yukki, riding included," taunted Ben.

"And I've already told you that I hate riding, I only do it because Mum makes me," added Charlie.

I was suddenly possessed by rage. "I haven't seen you ride," I told him, "but if you're as bad at it as the other two, I'm not surprised that you hate it. What they do isn't riding, they haven't the first idea, they think all they have to do is kick and haul. Riding is a skill, not a matter of sticking on and, for the pony's sake, you should at least learn to sit correctly and give proper aids." The Sternes stared at me and I guessed I was being compared unfavourably with the despised Delia, but I was too angry to care. I turned Tarka loose and took myself off to the tackroom without another word.

By the time all the horses were settled for the night and I had cleaned four bridles and two saddles, I felt exhausted and convinced that I was a total failure in my first job. But a delicious dinner of stuffed pancakes, pigeon pie and lemon sorbet, which Lisa produced with the air of a magician, revived me. She didn't seem very interested in my complaints about the children's riding, but when I began to talk about the Sterne treasure she became attentive at once.

"Perhaps that's what my prowlers were after," she suggested. "Only I don't think an elderly solicitor would really search for treasure at two in the morning."

"And you'd have heard the metal detector," I reminded her. "Unless of course he'd found a hopeful site with the detector earlier and then come back after dark to dig."

"Bringing one of his mates," added Lisa. "Remember that I heard two voices."

"But you didn't see any sign of digging?" I asked.

"Never looked," she answered. "But treasure-seekers would be good news, because if they've tried and failed they won't be back. I don't want to sleep with my window shut all summer."

FOUR

On Wednesday morning I groomed all the horses up to
Kingsdown standard, bandaging tails and oiling hoofs,
and I even made a start on pulling Rufus's straggling
mane.

As I worked I worried about the Sterne children. I
didn't want to make enemies of them, but I *was* supposed
to be improving their riding. I didn't think much would
be gained by insisting that they rode in the school—I
could see them sitting even more grotesquely than usual
in revenge—on the other hand I didn't want to be
despised as weak and wet like poor Delia.

The knights were another source of worry. At Kingsdown working pupils had not been encouraged to talk to
the paying clients. We had led horses out, tightened
girths, pulled down stirrups, and generally acted as
grooms, but the queries, complaints and chatting up had
been the province of Major Braithwaite and the two
instructors. Now it looked as though that was part of my
work too and I had a horrible feeling that I might be
speechless when confronted by three knights.

Building jumps for Tarka cheered me. I found fir poles on the woodstack, oil drums lying about everywhere and, thrown into a patch of nettles in the paddock, three pony-sized showjumps. I dragged them out, guessing that they were the coloured jumps Snowy had refused to face, and discovered that I had a gate, wall and road closed. Erected, they gave my course a much more professional air. When I had I marked out the school with the smallest size of oil-drum and arranged the thickest poles for cavaletti work, I felt that I was equipped for schooling and, even if the Sternes had no wish to improve, Tarka and Rufus would profit.

Tarka seemed a reformed character. He made no attempts to bolt off and, with a little prompting, he remembered how to turn on the forehand. He was circling well so I began to teach him leg-yielding, an exercise much practised at Kingsdown, and then we tried trotting over the poles. He was brilliant at this, lowering his head, rounding his back, and lengthening his stride in the approved manner and he seemed proud of his new skill and pleased with my pats and praises.

He enjoyed jumping the course even more. I began with the fir pole and oil-drum jumps, and, when he flew all of them, I circled and went on over the show jumps. At their lowest heights they were nothing to him and he jumped them with obvious ease and pleasure. I dismounted, rewarded him with a handful of oats, and made a fuss of him.

At least I was being successful with one pupil, I told myself. Perhaps my next job should be schooling ponies rather than people, I thought as I led him towards the yard.

Ben and Felicity were waiting for me.

"We didn't know that Tarka could jump like that," said Felicity as they opened the gate.

"Coloured jumps too," added Ben, a faint note of respect in his voice.

"All horses will jump coloured jumps," I told him in my Kingsdown voice. "It's a question of training and being properly ridden."

Snowy won't," Felicity countered obstinately.

"Are you going for a hack?" I asked, seeing that their ponies were tacked up.

"Yes, we were waiting for you," answered Ben.

"But I've no horses to exercise; they're jousting. I was going to weed the yard."

"Oh do come with us, it's more fun if you're there," pleaded Ben. "You don't *have* to weed, Delia never did."

"We want to show you another ride," added Felicity.

Wondering if this was an olive branch, I weakened.

"O.K., I'll come on Tarka and see if he tries his tricks when we're hacking."

We set off across the park, right-handed and slightly uphill, heading for the pavilion and jousting ground.

"You have to call it the lists," said Felicity in her bossy voice. "Mr Melville gets very annoyed if we don't use the correct names for everything."

"Who cares about him?" asked Ben, waving his arms and legs wildly as he tried to manoeuvre Romany up to a hunting gate behind the pavilion. The gate opened into a spinney which ran along the inner side of the park wall. A narrow path, soft and silent with leaves and pine needles, led through the narrow belt of trees.

"Let's canter," suggested Ben. "It's a non-bolting-off

place even for Tarka."

The spinney took us to the far end of the park and we crossed a lane into a beechwood. It was literally carpeted with bluebells. An unruffled sea, deeply blue, stretched away on either side of us and the air was heavy with their scent.

"Look at that!" I exclaimed. "We do have them in Buckinghamshire, perhaps not quite so many, but you forget how beautiful they are between one spring and the next."

"You're glad you came then?" asked Felicity. "We thought this ride might put you in a better mood."

"Beautiful views, rushing rivers and bluebell woods do put me in a good mood," I agreed, "but hideous sights, like people riding badly, spoil my day."

"Let's have a trot," called Ben hastily.

We trotted and I did my best to keep my eyes on the beauties of the countryside and off the Sternes. Tarka behaved perfectly and didn't attempt to dash off even when I jumped him over a couple of fallen trees. The sight of the Sternes jumping tree trunks was terrifying, for with their legs stuck forward and their reins in loops, they were in no position to steer. When Ben and Romany had a near collision with a standing tree and Felicity had almost been swept off by a low branch, I decided that my nerves could take no more and hurried them away.

The wood brought us to a heath with short rabbit-cropped turf and a rich smell of sun-warmed herbs. In the midst of it was a hollow, probably an old chalk quarry, long disused and grassed over.

With Tarka going so well, I couldn't resist a little

showing off and, calling to the Sternes to put their legs back, shorten their reins and follow, I rode down the most gentle of its sloping sides. They didn't follow. I rode Tarka out and in again, this time at the trot and then again at the canter.

"I wonder if we could turn it into a sort of Badminton Quarry with jumps," I suggested when I rejoined them. "You could have the most marvellous cross-country course here; it's such a waste that none of you want to be event riders."

"If you don't come on, we'll be ages late for lunch, and that'll put Lisa in a bad mood too," Felicity complained resentfully.

She was right, so we trotted on briskly until we regained the park and then, as we walked the last lap home, I reopened the subject. "I used to long to be in the Pony Club horse trial team," I told her. "It was my dream for about three years. But of course it was hopeless. I didn't have a pony of my own, we couldn't afford one, and no kindly farmer or rich landowner offered to lend me one as they do in pony books."

I looked at her unresponsive face. "Don't you have dreams of being chosen for the team and riding to victory?" I asked.

"No, you don't understand, the last thing we want is to be like the Pony Club people. We went to a rally once and it was really loathsome. We hated everyone: the instructors were bossy and all the children were so pleased with themselves."

"But you're pleased with yourselves," I protested. "You're proud that you ride badly. I think it's pathetic. How can anyone be proud of doing something so badly that they spoil a good pony like Tarka."

After this outburst we finished our ride in disagreeable silence. I tried to console myself for having lost my temper *again* with a lunch of two scrambled eggs on toast, followed by a banana and a fruity choc bar. Then I attacked the weeds. They had made a deep green matted carpet all over the cobbled yard, but, being shallow rooted, they were quite easy to pull up. I was just trundling my first wheelbarrow load towards the muck-heap, when a vague-looking man slipped furtively through the gate into the yard. At first I thought he was a knight and I was about to ask which horse he owned, when I saw the Sterne dogs at his heels and recognised the pale hair and thick spectacles. He wasn't as square or as pink and white as Charlie, but I guessed he was the children's father.

"You must be Kate Winton," he said looking everywhere but at me as he shook my hand. "I'm Mr Sterne. "You're doing a great job here, yes a great job. Tremendous."

"Thank you," I answered.

We both stood there embarrassed by our silence.

"Is everything all right?" asked Mr Sterne. "I mean do you have everything you need?"

"I could do with a new broom. Look," I seized my opportunity and displayed the balding broomhead.

"It's certainly seen better days," admitted Mr Sterne.

"And if you have a spare map, one with the bridle paths marked on it, I'd love to borrow it, please."

"I'll see what can be done," he muttered, avoiding my eye.

"Have you seen Mr Melville about? I'm supposed to

be meeting him here. We have a few points to discuss before the practice."

"Not yet, but I'm expecting all three knights. I'd better empty this wheelbarrow," I told him and made my escape. Then, seeing that he was still peering round the yard in a vague and helpless manner, as though expecting Mr Melville's head to appear over a loosebox door, I occupied myself with squaring the muckheap.

When Mr Melville did arrive by car which he parked outside the garages, he was wearing breeches and boots and carried a small suitcase. I left the two men talking—Mr Melville seemed to be doing most of it—and slipped away to the cottage to have tea and change into my more respectable jeans.

The second knight to arrive was tallish and gangling with short, spiky fair hair. He looked about twenty and his face, which was on the long side, wore a rueful smile for he had just realised that he was leaving a trail of horse caparisons and knightly gear across the yard.

"Hi, I'm Chris, Chris Clarke. The comedian of this outfit."

"Kate Winton," I answered, picking up a balaclava helmet, knitted in silver and grey wool, and restoring it to the pile in his arms.

"Is it still O.K. to change in the spare loosebox?" he asked.

"Yes, as far as I know."

"Great, I'll get changed before I caparison Rufus." As he vanished into the empty loosebox the third knight came strolling in. He carried his gear efficiently in a designer sportsbag and I noticed at once that he was good-looking. He was about the same height as Chris, but not in the least gangling. I guessed him to be older —about twenty-five. His hair was dark brown with chestnut highlights, and grew crisply, not curly, but in attractive swirls. His eyes were dark blue and rather deepset, his nose was straight while his well-shaped mouth had a determined, slightly unapproachable look.

Stunning, I thought, and hurried towards the tackroom, but Chris, pulling a green and gold tabard over a loose garment of knitted chainmail, called me back. "Come and meet Mark."

"Kate Winton meet Mark Chandler, our star performer. Have you heard that she's taken over the stables?" he asked.

"No, but that's splendid." Mark, shaking my hand, suddenly smiled. "You're the A.I., the professional we've been promised. That's wonderful news and I must say I noticed the difference in the yard at once."

Dazzled by the smile, I muttered something about having removed a few weeds and then stood feeling stunned and stupid until Chris called.

"Kate can you come and hold Rufus? He doesn't take kindly to all this dressing up."

As he caparisoned Rufus in an enormous horsecloth—green braided with gold—which reached almost to his fetlocks, Chris talked and I tried to recover from the stunning Mark.

"This is new," he said smoothing the horse cloth before girthing the saddle over it. I'm the green knight, not as judgmental as the one who took off Sir Gawaine's head, but a sound, ecologically-minded chap. Now, we have to get this headpiece over the bridle. We don't normally practise in full gear, but this evening's a dress rehearsal and any problems which emerge have to be sorted out by Sunday."

By the time the knights were dressed and the three horses caparisoned, Mr Sterne had returned with the children and they were loading lances, spears and other mysterious objects into the Range Rover.

"Mum says we have to do this to earn our keep," complained Charlie as I went to help him manoeuvre three very heavy lances out of the spare loosebox and into the car. "On Sunday it's going to be far worse, we've got to dress up as pages."

"You'll have to dress up too," Felicity told me. "Even Dad's got to because he's giving the commentary. They're letting him off with a cloak and a velvet hat with a plume round it, but he's still furious; he hates that sort of thing."

"Look at *this*." Ben thrust a decapitated human head at me and shrieked with delight when I recoiled. A second look told me that the gory-looking head was made of polystyrene.

'What's it for?" I asked.

"It's the head of an enemy, I've got a whole sackful here," Ben told me with relish.

"The knights spear them, they're given points for each one carried." Charlie made it sound very matter of fact.

As Mr Sterne drove the laden Range Rover to the lists, Mr Melville, resplendent in a dark red tabard and carrying a red shield emblazoned with a rearing dragon in gold, marshalled the rest of us.

"Charlie and Ben, you will have the responsibility of leading the cavalcade," he announced, "so you must set a good pace. No dawdling or chattering. You have to enter into the spirit of the joust and remember it's a great

honour to have all these noble knights around; rather
like having the Queen to open the village fête.

"Kate and Felicity will follow you. I'll follow them
and Mark and Chris will follow me, as a pair. Any questions?"

"Yes, last week you said that we were going to carry
flags," Felicity reminded him.

"And so you are, yellow banners with the Sterne crest,
but they're not quite ready so perhaps you could rehearse
with sticks or poles."

As the Sternes rushed off to find flag substitutes, Mark
Chandler, who had strolled over to listen to our briefing,
said, "Sounds as though we're going to be a bit thin on
the ground compared to the Lyme people."

"We certainly can't compete with them numerically,"
Mr Melville answered. "But they have been established
for some time. There's no doubt our first priority is now
to double our numbers. I think I've found a new recruit
and I hope you and Chris will do the same."

When the knights were fully dressed and mounted the
change in them was really impressive. Their helmets,
plumed and crested, made strangers of them, for all we
could see were their eyes. Tall and magnificent with the
simulated chainmail looking surprisingly like the real
thing and the richly coloured tabards glowing in the setting sun, they followed us up the park. Reins in one
hand, pennant in the other and the shield on the pennant arm, they tried to control their prancing horses.
Fiesta, a fairy tale Arab, caparisoned in blue and gold.
Marmaduke, formidable and splendid in his crimson red.
Rufus looking positively handsome, now that his ewe
neck and narrow frame were concealed by green and

gold drapes.

On reaching the lists the knights gave us their shields, pennants and helmets, which Felicity told me bossily I must call helms, and began to exercise. The Sternes and I unloaded the car, stacking the spears and lances against a sort of outsized knife rest made of fir poles.

"This is our end," Felicity told me. "The Knights of Lyme have another rack at their end. Now can you help with the quintains; we're not really tall enough."

The quintains, which were wooden shields attached to swivelling arms, had to be slotted on to posts on either side of the tilt and fitted with heavy metal balls on chains. Charlie explained that these acted as counter-weights, swinging the shields back into position after they had been struck by the knights' lances.

"If the knights ride too slowly the weights can hit them," Charlie went on," and Mr Melville says that in medieval times they often used bags of flour instead of metal counterweights and when the bag burst over a jouster the audience thought it was brilliantly funny and all fell about."

"Not surprising," I said. "If you were a ragged peasant, and had to keep holding horses and bowing politely to toffee-nosed knights; it must have been great to see them looking silly."

Our knights were cantering round and round the tilt, a long white fence, about one and a quarter metres high with a smooth and continuous rail, which ran along the top of the posts as they do at racecourses, while a criss-cross of latticework filled in the space below. Mr Sterne was making nervous announcements on the micro-phone. Then, stuttering slightly, he began to read out the biography of that noble knight Sir Walter Melville.

"None of it's true," Felicity assured me. "Mark is called Sir Marc, with a C, de Salis and he's supposed to be of royal French blood, that's why he has gold fleur-de-lis on his shield. Chris wanted to be the illegitimate son of a king or prince so he's called himself FitzCharles, Sir Christian FitzCharles."

When Mr Sterne announced that the performance was about to begin, Felicity and Ben stationed themselves by the rack to hand out lances and Charlie and I were sent to control the quintains. They were opposite each other, half way along the tilt fence, but on the outside of the track, and we had to crouch down on the far side of them and keep the wooden shields steady by holding the counterweights. The moment a knight struck we had to let go and then bring the shield back into position for the next knight.

When they began to race round the tilt, one behind the other, the thunder of hoofs, the crack of a lance that had found its target and the sight of the quintains swinging wildly would have been exciting, but for the fact that Chris kept missing. I felt full of sympathy for him as he tried to control the stargazing Rufus with one hand and wield a heavy lance in the other, but there was no doubt that he ruined the show. Mr Melville only missed once and Mark, looking wonderful with his hair blowing in the breeze—he had discarded his chainmail headgear with his helm—scored every time. They didn't offer Chris any helpful advice, but just shouted. "Bad luck!" or "Have another go," as they swept by.

When the quintaining ended Charlie and I had to take the shields down and hang a collection of large metal rings from the swivelling arms. A rather breathless Mr Melville explained that on Sunday there would be a single-stick fight by two of the men of Lyme to amuse the spectators while we set up the lancing of the rings and the horses had a breather.

Mark was brilliant at the rings and Mr Melville announced proudly that he had scored a personal best, so once again the despondent person was Chris, who had only carried three.

Having bullied Mr Sterne into announcing a sword fight between two of the men of Lyme, Mr Melville explained that on Sunday, while this was in progress, Charlie and I would collect the rings and Felicity and Ben would put the heads in two heaps, one on either side of the tilt.

Then poor Mr Sterne, sounding deeply embarrassed, had to read out a long piece about the history of head-spearing. Apparently the Turks, or Infidels, had had a custom of playing football with the heads of their enemies after battles and the Christian Crusaders, not to be outdone, had taken to decapitating the Turkish dead and using *their* heads for spearing practice.

We handed out the spears, which were much lighter than lances, and Mark rode into action. Galloping down the tilt, he speared a head and waved it aloft in triumph. Reaching the far end, he shook it off his spear, turned, and then, as he raced back to us, speared another. Chris speared one too, but, while we cheered, with relief rather than triumph, it fell off his spear and, as he hadn't carried it for four lengths, it didn't count. Mr Melville improved with practice, Mark remained consistently brilliant, but Chris grew worse, for Rufus became less controllable as he hotted up.

As Felicity and Ben returned the gruesome heads to
their sack, Charlie and I handed out helms and the heav-
ier lances and Mr Sterne told an imaginary audience that
we were now coming to the thrilling climax and were
about to witness the dangerous and dramatic sport of
jousting. Reading without much expression, he was
making it all sound rather low-key and I could hear Mr
Melville tut-tutting testily inside his helm, as he listened
to his dramatic prose being ruined.

The helms, which were heavy and padded inside to fit
a particular knight's head, were elaborately decorated
with plumes or crests. I'd expected them to have visors,
but instead there was a narrow opening through which
only the eyes were visible.

"Can you see where you're going?" I asked Chris as
the other riders lined up, Mr Melville at our end and
Mark representing the Knights of Lyme.

"Straight ahead, tunnel vision," he answered. "And
the shield is another problem, but even more essential, as
is about to be demonstrated."

The two knights thundering towards each other were
an impressive sight. They rode on opposite sides of the
tilt fence, their lances slanted across it.

"They have to try to strike each other on the top outside corner of the shield," Chris explained. "A strike on
the inside is dangerous, the lance can shoot up and get
the other bloke in the face, and a strike in the centre can
unhorse one or both of you, with painful consequences,
or break the striker's wrist. Brilliant!" he shouted as the
knights met with a clash of lance on shield. "A double
strike that means they both score."

Chris rode against the other knights, but weighed down by lance and shield and riding one-handed, he had little control. Instead of riding a straight course, he and Rufus swerved about and their opponents thundered by without attempting a strike.

"Mustn't go for a strike unless you're in a good position," Mr Melville, out of breath again, told us as he pulled up. "You can lose points for an incorrect or dangerous strike."

"You're absolutely right about the need for new recruits," Mark told him as we watched Chris careering across the park on a wildly stargazing Rufus. "I can't see poor old Chris making much of a show and you and I can't carry him on our own."

The Sternes were gloomy too. "The Lyme knights are good." Charlie told me, as we loaded the Range Rover at the end of the practice. "They'll massacre our lot."

"Does it matter who wins?" I asked. "I though it was supposed to be a spectacle rather than a contest."

"Right, but Chris isn't much of a spectacle," observed Charlie, "and the Lyme lot have more people than we do so they won't be pleased if we can only give them two proper jousts." "And if we don't have attractions the house attendances will go down and we'll be out in the street, at least that's what Mum says," added Ben in an even gloomier voice.

The knights stabled their horses and packed up their gear. Mr Melville announced that they must all practise at every available opportunity and that he would put in an hour in the morning. Mark gave me a brilliant smile as he dumped his tack on the saddle horse and said, "I must dash. Sorry not to help, Kate, but I have a dinner engagement, boss's wife needed an extra bloke; couldn't get out of it.

"Night, see you," he called to the others as he hurried to his car.

The Sternes faded away as soon as the Range Rover was unloaded and I found myself contemplating three sweaty saddlemarks, three hungry horses and a pile of dirty tack.

I'll never get through by nine, I thought dismally, and Mrs S. did say that the knights cleaned their *own* tack on summer evenings.

I was sponging out Marmaduke's saddlemark and still feeling hard done by—one trouble about working with horses is that you can't take your anger out on them—when Chris looked over the loosebox door.

"I've brushed Rufus over and topped up his water. Has Mark scarpered?"

"He said he had a dinner party, with his boss."

"Typical. Shall I do Fiesta while you sort out the feeds?"

"Oh yes, please." Finding that I hadn't been totally deserted was cheering and, with the horses settled, I approached the mountain of dirty tack decisively. "I'm not doing the children's, it's bad for their characters," I told Chris, "and the rest is only getting a lick and a promise."

"Good thinking," he said, breaking a bar of chocolate and handing me half," I hope you're getting double time for this,"

"No hope of that," I told him, "the Sternes are far too broke."

We raced through the tack cleaning without talking

much, I was feeling exhausted by the long day and Chris seemed rather downcast, which was hardly surprising after his disastrous performance. At five minutes to nine I said the rest must wait and ran for the cottage, but I was still changing into a clean sweater when Lisa appeared with our dinner. She was furious to find the table unlaid. Banging dishes and muttering angrily about a ruined souffle, she seemed to think that it was my fault the jousting had ended so late.

"But Mr Melville's in charge," I protested. "And Mr S. was there; I can't boss them around."

"You could remind them that dinner's at eight, eight sharp," she snapped at me.

As we ate our first course, which owing to the inability of soufflés to be kept waiting was baked eggs, Lisa's anger cooled and, halfway through the *coq-au-vin* she enquired how the practice had gone.

"I've never seen jousting before, so I'm no expert, but Mark Chandler seemed brilliant, Mr Melville efficient and poor Chris Clarke quite useless."

"Yes, that more or less confirms the Sterne verdict. Mr S. was deeply depressed at dinner, he thinks they've backed a loser."

"The knights were depressed too. They're trying to find new recruits, but meanwhile everyone's worried that there'll be a fiasco on Sunday."

"Can't you do something about this Chris?" asked Lisa. "They say he's a rotten rider."

"It's not *altogether* his fault," I told her. "I don't see how anyone can joust on an unschooled horse and Rufus is worse than unschooled: he's a stargazer and charges about with a stiff back and his head so high that

his ears are practically in your face. He's terrified of the
bit, he doesn't accept it or your legs at all."

Lisa's intelligent brown eyes, gazing from behind the
enormous glasses, seemed to hold more respect for me
than usual.

"You obviously know something about it, so what do
you plan to do?" she asked.

"Me," I looked at her doubtfully. Tarka was one thing,
but I didn't see myself re-schooling the knights' horses.

"Yes, you're in charge aren't you? If I have problems
with the dinners I can't pass the buck, there's no one to
pass it to, I have to sort it out myself and you're in the
same position with the horses."

I thought back to Kingsdown. I knew that Helen and
Klaus would have insisted that it was a three months' job.
I could hear Klaus's slightly Germanic voice. "Schooling
a horse is the same as training an athlete or even a ballet
dancer. You cannot force him to carry himself well. You
must build up the muscles, you must make him strong,
even change his shape and then he will be able to obey
and to carry out the movements. It takes time."

"Rufus is a mess, it'll take three months to put him on
the bit and build up the muscles of his neck and quarters," I told Lisa.

"No short cuts?" she asked.

At Kingsdown short cuts were forbidden, but then
they had the best of materials, beautiful young horses
and even the spoiled ones were full of potential. At
Croome Hill the ponies were bought at bargain prices
and, as they had to earn their keep, were often ridden by
the better pupils during their re-schooling. I remember
an excitable grey, Silver. He had star-gazed and Marian

had put him in a vulcanite pelham. Pelhams were frowned on at Kingsdown—something to do with the downward action of both reins—but it must have worked on Silver, for two years later he had become the local Pony Club dressage champion.

"I'll have a go," I told Lisa. "He's so ghastly that I don't think I can possibly make him worse. I'll get Chris to try a different bit. Or I might have a look through those chests in the tackroom first. Felicity says they're full of her Great Aunt Hermione's tack and no one's opened them for years."

FIVE

That night, I emerged from my usual deep sleep to find Lisa, ghostly in a white Victorian-style nightie, shaking me.

"Wake up, Kate. Come on, for goodness sake wake up. They're here again," she whispered in a frightened voice.

"Who's here?" I asked sleepily.

"The prowlers," she shook me impatiently. "Don't say anything *listen!*"

I listened. There was no sound. No wind rustling, no owls hooting, no scrape of iron-shod hoof. I crawled reluctantly from my bed and followed Lisa, who was creeping towards the kitchen window. She lifted the cor-.ner of the red-checked curtain cautiously. We both peered into the darkness.

"They've gone and you didn't hear them," I knew from Lisa's voice that she felt cheated.

"No, they haven't. Look." I pointed at a circle of dancing light in the stableyard. "That's a torch." The darkness, unrelieved by moon or street lamps, was dense

66

and black. Staring into it I couldn't see the shape or shadow of the torchholder.

"They're planning to steal the horses, or the tack," I said, suddenly wide awake. "Where are my shoes?"

"Don't be silly," Lisa grabbed my arm. "You can't go out there. They might attack you."

"But we can't let them take the horses. They'll have them in France or Holland being slaughtered for meat in a matter of hours. None of them are freeze-marked," I told Lisa as I tried to force my feet into her boots which were several sizes too small.

"No, look, they're going. The torchlight is moving into the paddock. Open the door, then we'll be able to hear if they start a car."

We opened the door without turning on the lights and stood outside, both shaking with a mixture of fear and cold. But as the dancing beam of light moved steadily across the paddock, the darkness grew less threatening.

"They must have left their car on the road then," said Lisa, as we turned back into the cottage. I switched on the light as she locked and bolted the door.

"Shall I make some tea?"

"Yes, and let's have the fire, I'm frozen."

Dressing-gowned and warm, we sat drinking tea and worrying about the prowlers' intentions until dawn, and then, as the sky lightened to grey and a bird broke the silence with the first solo of the dawn chorus, we felt brave enough to fall into bed.

Over breakfast I was able to report that none of the horses or tack was missing, and we agreed that Lisa should speak to Mrs S.

"She'll have to take me seriously now you've seen them too." Lisa sounded relieved. "But what she can do, I don't know. We need a telephone."

"Haven't they a cordless one they could lend us," I suggested.

"I've told you the poor dears live in a time warp, they don't go in for mod cons. Anyway, we're too far from the Castle—a cordless one wouldn't work."

"She could tell the police."

"They won't be interested until we've *been* attacked. But it's odd," Lisa went on thoughtfully, "last week it was talking which woke me, but this time they were silent; it was only the click of the gate that gave them away."

"Perhaps there was only one of them," I suggested.

"Could be, or they may have realised the cottage is inhabited. It had been standing empty for several weeks when I arrived."

Great Aunt Hermione's chests were another time warp. I unlocked the first one nervously—the prowlers had made me consider the possibility of a dead body as well as mice and moths—but it had been most efficiently packed with sheets and sheets of ancient newspapers and it reeked of camphor balls. To my disappointment it was full of rugs. Thick elegant day rugs, dark blue with red binding and the Sterne crest in the corner. Not much use to us, I thought, though at the bottom there were two newish stable rugs and four summer sheets, which might come in handy.

The second chest smelled of leather and neatsfoot oil. Reins, stirrup leathers, nosebands, martingales and breastplates were all packed in tidy newspaper parcels. I dug deeper and found stirrup irons and, finally, bits. I emptied a canvas bag of bits on the tackroom floor and there, among the driving bits, the snaffles, the bridoons and curbs, were several pelhams and one was exactly what I wanted: a vulcanite pelham with a good thick mouthpiece. Like everything else in the chests, it was Highland pony size and would fit Rufus.

Excited at the prospect of trying out the bit, I abandoned Kingsdown standards and gave the three horses a very sketchy groom. I was saddling Rufus when Felicity and Ben appeared.

"Can you come and catch Tarka, please," Felicity asked, "and if you're going for a hack we'll come with you."

"I'm going to school Rufus and then Tarka, but I'll hack at eleven if you like," I answered."

"You're always schooling," complained Ben. "We want to go for a really long ride—a picnic ride—with our lunches."

"O.K.," I agreed, "I'd like that, but you must give me some warning; I have to fit it in with the knights."

I walked Rufus on a loose rein for a long time, trying to persuade him to relax and to accept my legs instead of rushing away every time they touched him. Then I took up a contact with his mouth and tried trotting. He was certainly less frightened of the pelham and didn't stargaze as wildly as he had in the jointed snaffle. I trotted round and round, trying to settle him into a regular rhythm and to bring down his head by using my legs quietly and firmly every stride. Then I tried very slow and gentle halts. They seemed to help because I would start off again with his head in the right place and try to keep it there with my legs. Each time I felt I was losing him, I would turn or circle or try a slight shoulder-in, anything to keep him on the bit. My legs began to feel as though they were about to drop off, but I did seem to be having some effect. I could see that neck muscles which Rufus hadn't used for years, if ever, were gradually beginning to work. Reminding myself that I mustn't go on too long or ask too much. I was patting him and making him walk out on a loose rein when the hearty voice of Mr Melville hailed me from the gate.

"Good morning, Kate."

"Good morning," I called, trying to sound more enthusiastic than I felt, for, with Tarka to school before my hack with the Sternes, I had no time for chatty knights.

"What a transformation," roared Mr Melville even more heartily and then, in a quieter voice as I approached, "It didn't take you long to spot the weak link in the chain. Do you think you can perform a miracle by Sunday?"

"No," I shook my head. "He's beginning to go on the bit at the trot, but at the moment it needs both hands and a lot of concentration to keep him there. He won't be easy to ride until the muscles of his neck and quarters develop, and he learns to use his back; that's going to take weeks, if not months."

"Well you're obviously on the right track, so keep it up." said Mr Melville, his heartiness temporarily subdued.

"You don't think Chris will mind my schooling Rufus?" I asked.

"Of course not he'll be delighted. He's a nice lad and it must be obvious to him that he's letting the side down."

"One of the problems," I said trying to put it tactfully, "is that he rides with his lower leg too far forward and, if he can't use his legs, he has no hope of putting Rufus on the bit. I don't like to tell him, I mean I'm younger than he is and only an A.I. ."

"Oh, you mustn't hesitate to give him a few tips. When I met him at a riding club 'do' and asked him along I didn't realise that he was such an inexperienced rider, whereas you've trained at *Kingsdown*. We all accept that you're the expert."

"I wouldn't rate myself that high," I told him as I dismounted and he opened the gate.

Mr Melville seemed quite happy to tack up his own horse so, as soon as I had put Rufus away, I made a dash to the woodstack for poles and then to the barn where I found a couple of stout wooden boxes which would make excellent supports. Another search of the nettles produced four more oil drums, so my course grew longer and I was able to build a combination and to convert two of the straight fences into spreads. It was a well spaced out course, which I hoped would encourage the smooth and fluid style which Kingsdown had drummed into us was so important for young horses. There, only the very experienced horses had been asked to make sharp turns or cut corners.

I was pleased with Tarka. He was becoming much more supple, his circles and shoulder-in were improving by the minute and he was no longer making dashes for the gate. Best of all, he now seemed to enjoy being ridden. He made no difficulties about jumping the new course. I steadied him when we came to the combination, and he seemed to grasp the problem very quickly, standing back for the gate and then lengthening his stride for the spread which followed. As we landed over the last jump there was a burst of clapping, and looking towards the gate I saw I had a new audience. Mrs Sterne was standing between Felicity and Charlie. I dismounted and led Tarka over.

"Extraordinary," said Mrs Sterne. "I don't know why the children can't manage him. He looks like a show jumper when you ride him. Now, I've got to rush," she went on before I had time to answer. "I just came down to say that I do want Charlie to go on with his riding and, since he hates Tarka so much, could he take turns on Romany with Ben?"

I looked at Charlie, grim-faced and silent, but dressed for riding. "Yes, of course, it's fine by me," I answered, "and if we could ride in the school sometimes. . ."

"Poor Mum's got to rush," Felicity interrupted hastily. "We're groomed and tacked up and we thought we'd show you the river path ride."

I changed to Fiesta and then, as we rode across the paddock to the west drive I inspected Charlie. He was really too big for Romany and he sat quite as badly as his brother and sister, but in an entirely different way. Leaning forward with his hands resting on his pony's withers, he looked insecure and utterly miserable. I tried to work out what was wrong. His knees seemed too low and the line that should run vertically through a rider's shoulder, hip and heel simply didn't exist.

As Felicity had her usual battle with Snowy, waving arms and legs ineffectually in her attempts to shut the field gate, I dismounted and told Charlie, "You're not sitting correctly. Do you think you could bring your lower leg further forward, put your shoulders back and look up?"

"I know," he answered in a dispirited voice. "Everyone tells me that, but I don't seem able to alter it; I'm a useless rider, that's why I hate it so."

"I don't think you're useless." I tried to sound encouraging. "You just need sorting out. To begin with you're riding too long. Let's pull your stirrups up, about four holes, I think."

"But they're *supposed* to come below the ankle-bone when you hang your legs down," protested Charlie.

"Yes, if you're sitting normally, but you're not sitting, you're sort of perched. There, now you can see that the angles at the hip, knee and heel are much sharper," I went on, as I tried to manipulate his ramrod-stiff body into the correct position. "How does it feel?"

"Most peculiar," answered Charlie in a long-suffering voice.

Felicity had slammed the gate shut and was becoming restive, so I remounted and we trotted on, past the old bridge and the broken-down boathouse. I kept looking back at Charlie and telling him how well he was doing, but I could see by his martyred expression that he was unconvinced.

Then Felicity slowed up and rode beside me. "We're coming to the old water mill. It used to grind the corn into flour for all the farms for miles around, but now it's only used on Saturdays and Sundays when it grinds bags of organic flour for the visitors."

I looked obediently as Felicity pointed out the old stone building with a clapboard tower, which housed the machinery and hoists, and at the mill pool, fed by the stream and controlled by a complicated series of weirs and sluice gates, which diverted water from stream to pool when needed.

"There's not enough water for everything," Charlie told me, as Felicity embarked on another of her gate-opening battles, "When our great-great-grandfather built the cascades he had to let the moat run dry, and the water in our part of the stream gets much lower when the sluice gates are opened and the water gushes in to turn the wheel."

We crossed the road beside the village bridge and rode on along the river bank. For a time all my attention was taken by Fiesta, who had convinced herself that wild animals lurked in the overgrown hedge which fenced the path, but when I looked back again, I was disappointed to see that Charlie was still tense and miserable. I began to wonder if I ought to advise Mrs Sterne to let him give up riding; after all it was supposed to be fun.

Then Felicity announced that we had come to the green lane.

"Even Charlie's O.K. to canter here, because the track's fenced and it's uphill all the way," she said, a slight note of contempt in her voice.

A glance at Charlie's anxiety-ridden face made me say no. "I don't think Charlie's used to his new seat yet— supposing we trot on ahead," I suggested. "Snowy won't mind waiting, will he? And then you can really gallop."

Felicity's planned ride proved too ambitious. I suddenly realised that if we went on to Wood End as she wanted, they were going to be terribly late for lunch, and I insisted on a shorter way home through the park.

We had an argument, but Charlie, who looked as though he were longing for the ride to end, backed me up.

After such an energetic morning, I gave myself a long leisurely lunch break, with soup as well as bread and cheese and bananas, before starting on the afternoon chores. I had cleaned most of the tack, done the stables and was filling haynets when Charlie appeared.

"I've come to help you turn out the ponies," he said. "The others are in Salisbury. They had to pay a second visit to the dentist. I was lucky not to have a single filling, but I've got good teeth. They're about the only good thing I *have* got." he added gloomily.

"Oh come on, that's not true, you're fishing for compliments," I objected. "I heard that you were a brainbox and a wizard with computers."

"Yes, I understand them, but Mum says if I only have solitary interests I won't make friends and then I'll end up a recluse like Grandfather."

"Haven't you many friends?" I asked, dumping the filled haynets outside the tackroom and collecting the ponies' headcollars.

"Not as many as Felicity and Ben. And no one here has much time for me, they're all too busy trying to make the estate pay."

"But you've got so much." I sought around for a tactful way of putting it. "You're privileged. You live in a castle in this lovely place; one day you'll be a lord, won't you?"

"Dad says not to count on it, they'll probably have abolished the House of Lords and hereditary titles before *he* gets it. And, if they don't I'll be about ninety so there's not much point."

We were about to turn the ponies out, when Chris appeared.

"Hi, Kate, hullo Charlie. He looked me. "Can I have a word?"

"Of course—shall we go into the tackroom?" I suggested wondering if he'd come to say I was never to school Rufus again. "What can I do for you?" I asked, hiding my nervousness with a brisk Kingsdown manner.

"Well, Walter phoned me at work to tell me what an extraordinary effect you were having on Rufus. He suggested and I agreed that it might be an idea for you to give me a lesson or two, you know teach me how best to ride him."

"A lesson or two," I repeated doubtfully.

"Well not if you're too tied up or it's too much trouble."

"It's not that," I assured him hastily. "The point is that I've only taught beginners or children before. I'm only an assistant instructor."

"Yes, but you were trained at Kingsdown. Walter was over the moon when he heard about that. He says it's the best and that you've been rubbing shoulders with the élite. Now, don't you think the time has come to pass on what you've learned?" He gave a wry smile. "And, since you have to start teaching adults some time; why not begin with a willing victim?"

"Well, if you're sure." I still didn't feel too happy about it. "When do you want to start?"

"Now, that is if you're free; if you're not doing anything tonight."

"Well, I'll feed the other two horses and have a quick cup of tea—would you like one?" I asked.

"No thanks, I had one at work, but I'll change and tack up while you have yours."

I gave the ponies some hay and then ate three chocolate brownies to sustain me through the ordeal and changed into a clean sweater to increase my authority. At Kingsdown they insisted on full riding gear, including hat and gloves, when instructing, but I decided that would look too formal in the Sternes' paddock.

Chris rode so appallingly that I soon forgot about him being my first adult pupil. I was too busy wracking my brain, trying to find a cure for the sorry picture he and Rufus made. It was a vicious circle: Rufus's stiff back meant that it wasn't easy to sit into him and use the legs to put him on the bit, and Chris bumping about with his legs stuck forward and trying to do everything with the reins, made Rufus's back stiffer and his stargazing worse.

I explained that he was a very difficult horse to ride—by far the most difficult of all the Sterne horses and ponies—and I told Chris about the vicious circle, adding that it is always the rider's job to break vicious circles; horses haven't the right sort of brains. Then as Chris was looking baffled, I turned him off and tried to demonstrate that if I could get Rufus to use his hindlegs, by using my legs at every stride, he would lower his head. Then I pointed out that his ears moved *away* from me as the top of his neck lengthened, and not nearer and nearer to my face as they did when he was stargazing.

Chris *said* that he understood, but he seemed incapable of putting his legs back and using them and, as he trotted round with Rufus's stargazing growing steadily worse, I could see that he was beginning to despair. I was despairing too, though I tried not to show it. Then I had an idea. Surely in Great Aunt Hermione's second chest I had seen a lungeing rein?

"I've got an idea, well two ideas really," I told Chris. "I don't think I can sort you both out at the same time, so I'm going to try to establish your seat by lungeing you on Rufus. But I think it would also be a great help if I could give you a lesson on a schooled horse. Would Mark lend you Fiesta?"

"He might, if I tell him what you're trying to do. If you really think it would help, I'll phone him tonight."

I found the lunge rein without difficulty, and cursing Great Aunt Hermione for not providing me with a cavesson and lunge whip, I substituted Rufus's headcollar and a beanpole from the woodstack. I didn't mind about side reins—at Kingsdown they were considered danger-ous in inexpert hands and A.I.s were not allowed to use them—but I thought of borrowing Fiesta's saddle.

"You'll find it a lot easier to sit correctly on this one," I told Chris as I took his stirrups away. Then I instructed him to sit deep and to keep his position by holding on to the pommel, and, knotting the reins, I told him he could pick them up if there were any problems.

Rufus had evidently been lunged before. He walked round happily while I nagged Chris into the correct position. Later we tried trotting and, once Chris got the idea of holding himself down, he began to look quite respectable.

"The legs feel most odd," he said, when I announced that he'd done enough for the first day. "Stretched in places where they've never been stretched before, but I could tell good things were happening. How long is it going to take to 'establish' this seat?"

"A few weeks," I answered, "and I'll be schooling Rufus at the same time."

"More shame on Sunday then," said Chris with his wry smile.

Charlie opened the gate for us.

"I hope you didn't mind my watching," he said to Chris.

"No, but it can't have been very exciting."

"Actually it was quite interesting, I've never seen a person lunged before."

"Nor have I," admitted Chris. "I learned to ride at one of those schools where the only instructions are 'Heels down,' and 'Kick him along'. All this is a great eye opener to me.

Is this stargazing my fault?" he asked as we put Rufus away.

"No, not unless you broke him in. I expect the tendency was there—he probably combined a weak neck with an excitable temperament." That was what the Martins had said about Silver.

"It's important to keep young horses very calm during their basic training, until they've developed the right muscles and become controllable." I went on. "If they become excited and the rider tries to control them by force, the clever ones may learn that they're stronger than their riders, which means you're in real trouble, while others, like Rufus, develop the wrong muscles and acquire bad habits."

"You mean that breaking-in is really a giant con trick practised against the entire equine race?" asked Chris.

"You could call it that. But since there are no prairies left to roam over, and being wild on a moor doesn't seem much fun, the best thing you can do for horses is to make it easy and comfortable for them to carry their riders and be good at something, so that they are valued."

"Well Fiesta certainly has an irritatingly smug expression, while poor old Rufus always look harassed, so they may prove your point," admitted Chris. "Now, if I can have a bucket of warm water, I'll do this tack."

Charlie, who was still hanging around in a lost sort of way, helped me turn the ponies out and then I told him he really must go home or he would be late for dinner.

"This lungeing," he said, looking at the ground. "It seems to be changing Chris. Do you think it would improve me?"

"Yes." I tried to hide my amazement that such a suggestion should come from a Sterne, especially from Charlie, whom I had expected to be suffering from pyschosomatic pains for the rest of the holidays. "Yes, I think it would. You're one of those people who find it hard to relax and hard to do several things at once. It might be exactly the right answer."

"Can we try then?" Charlie actually looked up at me. "I could come fairly early tomorrow morning—the others won't want to ride until later. Ben's got an 'I Spy' bird book and is determined to tick the whole lot off, so he's going out round the farms with Dad, and Felicity's helping Mum and Michelle unpack things in the shop."

"Would ten be early enough?"

"Yes, brilliant. And you won't tell the others?"

When I packed Charlie off and fetched Chris his bucket of warm water, I retreated to the cottage thinking I had time to answer a long letter from Mum before Lisa arrived with the dinner. I re-read the letter, thinking that

Mum's life was very dull compared with mine: the most world-shaking event seemed to be Robbie's new tooth and she asked a whole host of questions about Sterne. I set out to answer them, but had only managed half a page when, worn out by fresh air and exercise, I fell asleep.

Lisa was not pleased to find me sleeping and the table unlaid when she arrived with the *matelote bonne femme*— cod steaks and scallops on fried bread covered with a delicious sauce. As we ate she lectured me, saying that I must learn to pace myself, that no one could be expected to work a twelve hour day and if I was going to work in the evenings, I must do as she did and take a break in the afternoons.

"But Chris turned up without warning and asked for a lesson," I protested. "And everyone's desperate for me to do something about him and Rufus."

"Well insist that in future he books his lessons in advance," Lisa snapped at me. "No one appreciates *door-mats*."

"No, you're right. I must get the knights and children organized," I agreed meekly, thinking that though the saying advised people not to quarrel with their bread and butter, it was with the provider of *creme brulée* that I had to keep on good terms.

I had a feeling that Charlie's lungeing lesson was of vital importance, that he was clutching at a straw, and if it failed he would abandon riding for ever. So I went to sleep debating which pony to lunge him on, and awoke still uncertain. Snowy and Romany were both rather stiff and elderly and they didn't need the extra exercise. Tarka was the obvious choice, but Charlie was frightened of him and he might not be experienced on the lunge. In the end I settled on Rufus. I knew he was light, well balanced and obedient and, though taller than the ponies, his narrowness and lack of impulsion would prevent Charlie from feeling over horsed.

"Chris rang to say that he can borrow Fiesta, so he'll be over for his lesson at five," Charlie told me. He had appeared punctually, wearing jeans and carrying his jodhs, and disappeared into the spare loosebox, muttering that he was going to change. When I broke the news that he was to be lunged on Rufus, he turned a shade paler, but made no objections.

"You saw him yesterday, you know he goes well," I pointed out as Charlie heaved himself into the saddle; it was Fiesta's, which I decided to borrow again.

"Now, the knotted reins are there for emergencies, but there aren't going to be any," I told him as Rufus walked round. "All you have to do is to hold on to the pummel and think about your seat. Sit, don't perch, move about until it feels right.

Shoulders back. Good, now relax." When Charlie looked comfortable, I tried a trot and he was better than I expected. He seemed to have got the idea of holding himself down by the pummel and he was obeying my cries to sit deep, ride tall and look about him.

"This is the first time in my life riding without stirrups hasn't given me a stitch," he said, when I called Rufus in for a rest.

"That's because you're doing it properly. Riding ought to be smooth and easy. Horse and rider should move as one, with all the aids invisible."

"You make it sound quite poetic," said Charlie.

I stopped before he was tired by announcing that I must now school Rufus. "But you're doing brilliantly," I told him.

"Would you like another go tomorrow?"

"Yes please, it feels quite different from ordinary riding and I don't seem so bad at it—no worse than Chris."

"No, you're doing fine," I reassured him again.

The lungeing seemed to have done Rufus good too. He was calmer and more relaxed, until I introduced him to trotting over poles; he managed one, but two sent him into a sweating stargazing frenzy.

I schooled Tarka, accompanied Felicity and Ben for a short ride on Marmaduke, and was ready for Chris at five. He looked a lot better on Fiesta than on Rufus, and he found her a great deal easier to ride, but as he would not use his legs every stride, she soon lost her impulsion and began to look a very nondescript sort of horse.

"You must ride *forward*," I told him. "Use each of your legs in turn at the walk to make her walk out." But he couldn't seem to feel the rhythm of the walk so I tried the trot. Then my voice was ringing out like Helen's in a bad mood. "Come on, don't just sit there. Legs, both together, come on each time you sit down." But Chris looking long, lanky and feeble, went on letting Fiesta slop round, seemingly convinced that his legs could only be used to make a horse go faster.

I was about to confess myself beaten when I thought of trying the cross-country seat. I called him in and made him shorten his stirrups. "Now you don't stand up," I told him. "You have to concertina yourself by sharpening the angle of the hip, knee and ankle while your seat bones stay very close to the saddle. Shorten your reins. That's better. Keep your weight over your stirrups and your stirrup leathers perpendicular to the ground."

"But it's torture," groaned Chris. "I can't ride like this."

"Yes you can. Somehow I've got to turn you from a passive rider into an active one," I told him sternly. "Now keep those legs back and *use* them. Ride forward every stride."

It was hard work energising Chris—just as hard as schooling a horse oneself. I made him trot a large circle, change the rein and bend, come to a gentle halt, move off again, circle. I never stopped bullying him to use his legs, and gradually Fiesta came to life; she began to look as she did when Mark was riding her.

When Chris pleaded to stop I let him, because I was exhausted too.

"Do you understand about being an active rider?" I asked as he dismounted and groaned over the pain in his legs. "You don't just sit there, you ride forward every stride and if you want a rest you dismount. You never let your horse drift aimlessly around."

"I get the point," he said, "but whether I'll ever recover is another matter."

"It's easy when you get the habit and develop the right muscles," I comforted him. "At least on well-schooled horses like Fiesta it's easy; spoiled ones like Rufus *are* hard work."

We found Felicity and Ben sitting on the gate and giggling.

"We didn't know Kate could be so fierce," said Ben.

"Nor did I," agreed Chris. "She's the most ghastly

bully."

"But Fiesta did look quite different when you used your legs," Felicity told him. "Mark uses his O.K., doesn't he, Kate?"

"Yes, he's good, you don't see him waving his arms and legs around. He makes it all look easy, but you can tell by the way his horse goes that he's an active rider; he creates impulsion."

"We were wondering," said Felicity, with unusual diffidence, "whether we could change our minds and try riding in the school tomorrow?"

"But no riding without stirrups—it gives me the stitch," Ben interposed quickly.

"Of course," I answered Felicity. "What sort of time?"

"Could you school us together, tomorrow morning," suggested Chris. "It would be less work having us all at once, wouldn't it? I gather that Mark's bringing his prospective knight over in the afternoon—the idea is that Adrian rides Fiesta, Mark borrows Marmaduke and I act as their marshal."

"Right, at ten then," I decided. "And afterwards there'll be compulsory tack cleaning; we have to smarten the whole place up for the Knights of Lyme."

"Did you get a chance to talk to Mrs S. about the prowlers?" I asked Lisa as we ate duck—no—*canard a l'orange*, garnished with watercress.

"Yes."

"What did she say?"

"Nothing, she just sighed. I can see she thinks it's just one damn thing after another and with the Japanese tour organizer on her back, she can't cope. I did have a talk with the Whites, they reckon it's lovers who think they've found a nice quiet spot. But it's definitely not Michelle or Amy."

"But why should they come round by the stables? There must be lots of quieter places along the river bank."

"It's fairly marshy and they could be afraid of cows," Lisa suggested with a giggle. "And then we've got a little stone landing stage. It's overgrown, but useable, and there's an iron ring you can tie a boat to."

"But if they've got a boat they wouldn't come up the orchard and along the drive," I pointed out as I tried to make sense of it. "Is the main gate locked at night?"

"No, because it would mean someone would have to get up early and unlock it for the postman. But apparently the west drive and most of the field gates on the roads *are* padlocked."

"And there's no way from the hayfield into the orchard?"

"Only through a very scratchy hedge, or by the stream."

"It's a mystery. Did you mention the possibility of horse thieves or tack thieves to Mrs S.?"

"No, I've told you, she didn't want to know."

I dropped the subject then, because I could see that Lisa was getting edgy, but I resolved to have another look at the orchard next day and to suggest the possibility of freeze marking to the knights.

SIX

As I mucked out on Saturday morning I tried to prepare my lesson. 'Never go into the school without knowing what you are going to teach', they had drummed into us at Kingsdown. But there all instruction had been deadly serious, which might do for Chris, but would certainly not go down well with the Sternes.

At Croome Hill it had been quite different. Most people enjoyed the schooling days and I had preferred them to the rather tame hacks. But with classes of ten or twelve it had been easy to organize the light relief which had followed the serious work. I thought back to the excitement of team relay races, but bending and handy pony had been popular too and there had even been musical sacks with two lives each. I would adapt the Croome Hill approach, I decided. The reward for sitting correctly and riding in a civilized manner was going to be fun.

I could see that Felicity was rather annoyed when I told Chris to lead my tiny ride, but I began briskly, before she had time to complain, by asking them if they knew about overtracking. They didn't. So I explained that the walk was a pace of four-time, each hoof was put down separately and that the imprint of the hind hoof should always be in front of the one left by the fore hoof on the same side.

"Why?" asked Felicity.

"Because it shows the pony is using his hindlegs and walking out properly."

"Rom's not doing it," announced Ben hanging over his pony's side.

"Nor is Rufus," added Chris.

"If I use my legs, Snowy trots. Look," called Felicity, giving her pony a sharp kick.

"Of course he trots, you gave the signal to trot," I bawled at her. "If you want your pony to walk out you have to give the correct aid or signal. You ask him to walk out by pressing gently with the calf of each leg in turn in time with his stride. Relax, try to let your back swing with the walk and then ask each hindleg in turn to step out. *Gently*, Felicity. I shouldn't see your aids, I should only see the result of them."

"It works," called Chris in tones of triumph. "He's overtracking."

When I had persuaded Ben that it was possible to use the legs, sit up straight and still see the hoofprints. Romany began to overtrack. And finally, as soon as Felicity accepted that you didn't have to kick, Snowy began to stride out. We changed the rein and then with everyone overtracking I explained about correct bends on corners and got them to check that they could see the pony's inside eye and to make sure that they were *allowing* a bend by giving slightly with the outside hand. This caused a great shortening of Sterne reins.

Then we came to halting. I explained that it was a forward movement and when Felicity began to argue that it
couldn't be, I shouted, "Listen!" in my fiercest voice.
"When you halt correctly you ride your pony forward
into a stationary hand. You *don't* pull on the reins. A
good rider *never* pulls on the reins, he/she feels them.
Shorten your reins, Ben. Now, all stop your hands going
forward, but keep on riding forward until the pony
comes to a halt, standing squarely on all four legs as
though at attention."

No one got it right the first time, but when I had borrowed Snowy and demonstrated, they seemed to get the
idea and then I only had to shout, "Sit up", or "Look
straight ahead", at them.

When they had more or less mastered the halt, I
taught them the turn on the forehand—explaining that,
though it was rather a boring exercise, it was important
as it gave you control of the pony's quarters, but that
once he had learned to move away from your leg, you no
longer needed to practise it.

I was finding it rather difficult to fit my explanations
to Chris and Ben at the same time, but all my pupils
appeared to be enjoying their new power and the two
Sternes seemed amazed that such small, almost invisible
aids were willingly obeyed by their ponies.

I was feeling encouraged until I called for a trot then
all the improvement vanished. The Sterne legs shot forward, their hands shot up and my Klaus-like roars, about
perpendicular stirrup leathers and not seeing their toes,
were completely ignored. Chris on the other hand had
improved. He was trotting round in quite a steady

rhythm using his legs. I called the Sternes into the centre to watch him. But now he had a new problem. In his determination to put Rufus on the bit, he was setting his hands.

"You must keep a straight line from the bit, through your hand to your elbow," I told him. "You may think you're putting him on the bit by setting your hands below the level of the rein, but you're actually riding with the brakes on and *preventing* him from using his hindlegs."

Then, leaving Chris trotting large circles, I concentrated on the Sternes. I had decided on the cross-country seat cure so I made them pull their stirrups up and explained about sharpening the angles of the ankle, knee and hip. They set off round the school complaining loudly and their complaints grew louder still when I commanded a trot, but the effect on the ponies was extraordinary. Freed from lumpish riders bouncing about on their backs, they pricked their ears and began to move with much more spirit.

Charlie materialised beside me. "The ponies look different," he said. "It's been very interesting so far."

"Would you like a turn on Romany?" I asked, noticing that he was dressed for riding. "Ben's probably getting a bit tired."

Ben, saying that he wasn't tired, but that his legs were killing him, handed Romany over quite cheerfully and started to instruct his brother in everything he had learned so far. I hastily sent him to fetch ten beanpoles from the woodstack and, having checked the length of Charlie's stirrups, I told him to walk round until he was relaxed, and then worry about overtracking. Meanwhile

I had Chris and Felicity trotting large figures of eight, with a change of aids and bend in the centre of the school. When they were exhausted by the unaccustomed effort of using their legs, I sent them to put up the bending poles and watched Charlie halt, turn on the forehand, and trot round corners with the correct bend.

When I announced that schooling was over for the day and that we would now practise bending, Charlie turned green, Felicity began to kick and haul excitedly, while Ben demanded his pony back and Chris asked if it wouldn't be counter-productive for Rufus.

"We are going to do it slowly and correctly." I had to shout to be heard. "Now listen: you will trot up the posts riding as straight as you can, holding them away from the posts with your inside leg and outside hand. You will *not* steer round them as this slows the pony up. At the top you will halt and make a tight turn round the post, then trot back.

"Chris and Felicity first. Trot round in a large circle to get your ponies going, before you come to the start. Felicity, sit still! You slow Snowy up when you waggle your body and wave your arms."

Both riders had to have a couple of tries before I could convince them that a pony with impulsion didn't have to be steered round every pole. Then I sent Charlie against Felicity—he had obviously learned a lot from watching—and Ben with Chris.

"We're not racing," Felicity complained, as Ben and Charlie had a second go. "When are we going to gallop?"

"When we've taught the ponies how to do it properly," I told her. "Here, help me with these poles, I'm making a garden path." At Croome Hill garden path competitions belonged to the beginner's class and I hoped Chris wouldn't feel it was beneath him, but he seemed a very easy person who didn't worry much about his dignity.

The path between the poles was roughly a metre wide and I incorporated a couple of turns.

"Now, a hoof touching a pole is half a fault and a hoof outside is one fault," I told my ride. They all began to protest at once.

"It's too narrow."

"The corners are too sharp."

"It's all very well for Rom, but Snowy's too big to get round there."

"What about Rufus then? He's a hand taller."

"It's a test of whether you're using your legs at the walk," I told them calmly. "Get the ponies going with impulsion, use minimum steering and look where you *want* to go. Felicity, you can have first turn."

At first there was uproar as the riders insisted on using their reins and looking down at the poles and the ponies left the path at every corner, clocking up enormous numbers of faults. But gradually they began to use their legs and then to realise what a bad effect looking down had on their ponies.

When I announced that our time was up the Sternes all pleaded for more and Felicity wanted to jump.

"Next time," I told them. "I must feed Fiesta and Marmaduke now, or they won't have time to digest, and you all promised to clean your tack, remember? I don't want to be disgraced in front of the Knights of Lyme."

I smartened myself up during the lunch break, but,

when I looked in the mirror, I knew that giving my hair a quick shampoo and changing into a clean sweater and jeans hadn't put me on the same plane as Mark: I needed designer jeans and a Nicol Bruce sweater or at least some interesting garment picked up back-packing in Peru, which was how poor, but intelligent, people like Lisa got by.

Mark and Adrian Lewis arrived early in separate BMW's. Mark introduced us very formally and I took an instant dislike to Adrian. His black hair wasn't bad, but his nose was too large, his eyes too small and he had a little clipped moustache.

Finding that Chris hadn't returned from his lunch at the Sterne Arms, they decided to take a look at the Castle and left me to tack up the horses. As they weren't to be caparisoned, it wasn't a very arduous task, but I felt slightly aggrieved; obviously, when Mark had a friend with him, I was merely the groom. Chris was a much nicer character, I told myself, but then he hadn't Mark's looks or his accomplishments; I couldn't help being dazzled by that aura of success.

When Chris reappeared, he loaded his car with all the gear and then began tooting the horn for the missing knights. Eventually they returned and I gave Adrian the full Kingsdown groom service, tightening girths, pulling down stirrups and holding Fiesta, while he mounted. As they headed for the park, I could see that he was an experienced rider, and quite at home on Fiesta, while Mark looked unbelievably handsome on the prancing, champing Marmaduke.

I was contemplating a dash to the cottage to take off

my best sweater when Charlie materialized.

"Could you lunge me now, before the others come to clean tack?" he asked. "You did *promise* and there wasn't time this morning."

I felt like saying 'no', that he'd had his turn in the school, but I didn't. There was something almost desperate in Charlie's longing to be lunged when we all knew that he hated riding and I decided that if he needed attention that badly I had better give it to him.

"O.K.," I agreed. "Fifteen minutes and I don't suppose Chris will mind if we borrow Rufus again."

Now that Charlie knew how to sit, I made more transisitions from walk to trot and back again. I taught him some of the loosening up exercises and showered praise upon his smallest effort. Since anything new made him go stiff with anxiety we chatted a lot and I think he was quite sorry when his fifteen minutes were up.

I took off my best sweater for tack cleaning and, when Felicity and Ben turned up, all three Sternes worked hard, though they were inclined to quarrel over the one saddle soap sponge; no one wanted to use rags.

When they had finished the tack, turned out their ponies and gone to tea, I did a speedy evening stables and, changing back into my best sweater, took a mug of tea and a gingerbread out to the yard to wait for the knights. Chris drove in first.

"How did it go?" I called. He gave a thumbs up sign and began to unload. I went to meet Mark.

"Adrian's a natural, a perfect knight, and Fiesta went beautifully for him," he said, smiling and relaxed.

"For those kind words I thank thee greatly, Sir Marcus, and also for the loan of your warhorse," said Adrian, dismounting. I left him holding Fiesta, and took Marmaduke.

"What do I do, down sails?" he asked.

"If you mean unsaddle, yes please. How did Marmaduke go?" I asked Mark.

"He's a funny old lad, all that huffing and puffing and nothing much to show for it. He makes Fiesta seem like a Rolls, but still it was good of Walter to lend him."

"Is Adrian going to join the Knights of Sterne?" I asked as I wisped Marmaduke's saddlemark.

"I think he's tempted; he's going to mull it over this weekend. He has to decide between a boat and a horse, his salary won't run to both."

"He rides well?" I asked.

"Yes, he did quite a bit as a boy and now his firm's moving down here he's toying with the idea of taking it up again. He's in a different class from our Chris so he'd be doing us a favour if he joined."

Mark and Adrian vanished while I settled and fed the three horses, but as I was tidying up the tackroom, Mark reappeared, "Oh Kate, if you've finished, how about a drink at the local?" He asked. "Adrian's dashed off—a date in London, but I've time for a quick one."

"That would be great," I said, trying not to look as bowled over as I felt. "But are you sure, in these clothes?"

Mark smiled at me. "You look charming and it's only a country pub."

Chris emerged from the spare loosebox. "I've sorted out all the gear for tomorrow," he told us. "What about the tack, Kate?"

"I've done Rufus's and I'll have time for the rest

tomorrow," I answered. "I've refused to school the Sternes. . . ."

"She's clocked out and I'm taking her to the pub for a well-earned drink," Mark interrupted. "See you tomorrow, Chris."

He obviously doesn't want to make a party of it I thought, as Mark ushered me into the passenger seat of the silver BMW and I felt absurdly grateful that someone good-looking and sophisticated should want to drink with me. As he drove up the drive I made admiring remarks about the car, but by the time we had parked outside the Sterne Arms I had run out of conversation. I agreed to a vodka and tonic, which I didn't like much, but Mark was having one, and then we sat on an oak settle, in the corner of an oak-panelled room, decorated with coaching prints and horse brasses.

"To the Knights of Sterne," said Mark raising his glass and smiling at me. "Though I am afraid they will be disgraced tomorrow. It's infuriating, if only we could conjure up a horse for Adrian."

"Or a better one for Chris. I don't think anyone could do much on Rufus in his present state," I added.

"Poor old Chris—I think he's one of life's losers, but we mustn't take the knights too seriously. Tell me about your life. How do you get on with the Sternes?"

I soon realized that Mark wasn't interested in my accounts of the Sterne children, it was the Castle and the family history which intrigued him and he seemed rather shocked that I knew so little about it.

I asked where he had learned to ride so well and he explained that his people had farmed in Somerset and he had been a Pony Club boy and made all the teams in his time.

Then I asked what he did for a living and it seemed to be something to do with accountancy. He said he had been working in the City, but had decided to quit the rat race and work in Salisbury for less money.

When I talked about Kingsdown I could see his eyes glazing with boredom, but Lisa's stories of life in the Castle seemed to amuse him. I told him about her dress rehearsal for the Jacobean Banquet and how romantic the great hall had looked by candlelight: how the first floor bedrooms had all been done up with four-poster beds and private bathrooms for the tourists, while the family lived in squalor in the attics, and how Lord Sterne had a flat in the Armoury Tower above his beloved coin collection, and while the coins were comfortably housed in glass cases and kept at the correct temperature, Lord Sterne's flat had no central heating and he was said to watch television in his overcoat.

Over our second drink I told Mark about the prowlers and to my surprise he seemed tremendously concerned. "Why didn't you phone the police?" he demanded. And, when I explained that the cottage had no telephone he was even more horrified.

"You mean you've told the Sternes and they've taken no action at all?" he asked indignantly. "That's simply not on. I mean you two girls could be in danger and, since one gathers that there is nothing much of value left in the Castle, it has to be the horses they're after. I don't want to turn up one morning and find that Fiesta's on her way to an E.U. abattoir. Fiesta slaughtered and eaten, it's too horrible to think about." He covered his face with his hands. "And you say they haven't even padlocked the gate?"

"No, Mr White the gardener thinks it's lovers who've found a romantic spot by the river," I told him. "And it is true that they've been twice and so far nothing's been stolen. Still, I think we ought to padlock the tackroom door at night and it's really important that the horses should be freeze-marked."

"Oh no, I don't want Fiesta branded, she's far too beautiful," Mark objected. "All that's needed is to chain and padlock the gates. "Look, I'll phone Walter from the car and if he won't do anything I'll get on to the Sternes myself tomorrow."

"Oh thank you," I said, glad that someone was prepared to act. "It's rather a responsibility being in charge of so many valuable horses."

"I only wish I had a spare mobile phone I could lend you," he went on. "I really hate the thought of you girls alone in that cottage at night with no possibility of calling for help. There isn't a back entrance to the Castle; I mean you've no way of getting through into the shop or the snack bar?"

"No, there's a huge piece of the castle wall between us," I explained. "and as we can't even get from the barn into the garages, the only way to to the Castle is through the yard or by the stream. We could swim round—the stream's quite deep at the bottom of our orchard—and it's no distance. But I think we would have to tackle the thieves ourselves."

"No, that's definitely not on. Promise me, Kate, that you won't attempt any heroics. Fiesta means a lot to me, but I certainly wouldn't ask you to risk your life for her."

"She's such a perfect horse, sweet-natured as well as

being beautiful and well schooled. I don't think I *could* stand there and let her be stolen," I argued. "Supposing I put sugar in the horsebox petrol tank, let down its tyres, and then swim for help?"

Mark smiled his bowling over smile. "What a nice person you are," he said.

I was thinking the same thing about him, but I didn't say so, and he began to talk about holidays. He seemed to have been everywhere in Europe, and to Hong Kong and the USA on business. I had to admit that apart from a school trip to Spain and a weekend in Amsterdam I hadn't done much travelling. I didn't add that a chronic cash shortage had forced us to spend most of our holidays staying with Mum's aunt in Scotland.

Then the conversation seemed to falter and Mark, looking at his Rolex watch, said he ought to be on his way.

"I'll run you back to the stables," he offered.

"No don't bother. It's a lovely evening and I feel like a walk," I told him as we parted in the car park. He didn't kiss me, though I had half-hoped he might.

Walking up the drive, between the rows of chestnut trees which were just coming into flower, I suddenly felt happy. Really happy for the first time for months. I was a success at my job—well so far. The horses were great, Sterne was beautiful and there was Mark who actually liked me. Even the children were coming round to my way of thinking. Eighty-eight Holmwood Road seemed a long way away in a hazy distance, and somehow, not my problem.

I was contemplating the luxury of lying on the sofa with

a coffee and watching television until it was time for Lisa and dinner, when I noticed that the tackroom light was on looking in, I found Charlie, a lonely figure, laboriously saddle-soaping Marmaduke's bridle.

"What's going on?" I asked. "You did your tack this afternoon."

"Yes, I know. I came back to help you with the knights' tack, but you weren't here," he answered reproachfully.

"That was big of you," I told him, averting my eyes from the soapy froth that was collecting on Marmarduke's buckles. Somehow Charlie's saddle soaping was always too wet. "But isn't it nearly your dinner time?"

"Nearly. I've got ten minutes. Are you going to do Marmaduke's saddle?"

"Yes." I stifled a sigh at the loss of my television fix and got to work. "I was having a quick drink with Mark."

"Do you like him?" asked Charlie in a jealous voice.

"I don't really know him, he seems O.K.," I answered cautiously.

"Dad says BMWs are flash," observed Charlie. "And I hate people who are good at everything. Dad says it's O.K. to be really good at one thing, like Grandfather. Mum says you ought to have at least two interests, one indoors and one outdoors; what do you think?"

Realising that my opinion was important to Charlie, I thought hard, racing through all the people I had known at home, at school, at Kingsdown and Coombe Hill. "All-rounders probably have a better time, especially at school," I suggested, "but to be really brilliant at something you have to be single-minded. All the top tennis players and swimmers seemed to spend their whole lives training and famous musicians never stop practising. Even working with horses becomes a way of life. But I expect your mother's right, it's better not to specialize too early if it can be avoided."

"But with me it's not really a question of specializing, I've no choice. I'm simply no good at anything else," observed Charlie sadly.

"Oh come on, your riding's improved tremendously in a very short time," I told him in my most encouraging voice. "Perhaps you're one of those people who has to be taught. Some people pick things up naturally and others have to learn the hard way, but I don't think it makes much difference in the end."

"It makes a lot of difference at the beginning though," said Charlie ruefully.

SEVEN

At precisely ten o'clock on Sunday morning the little green-painted ticket office beside the drawbridge opened and the first cars came slowly down the drive to be shepherded into the public car park—a roped off section of the park—by Mr White.

I was grooming the three horses to Kingsdown standards, though I knew most of my work would be hidden by their caparisons. I had a feeling that the Knights of Lyme would come early to inspect the opposition and I was determined that, even if we were to be disgraced in the joust, we should be the better turned out team. I paid special attention to tails, for at least they would be visible to the spectators: Fiesta's was shampooed to a dazzling white, Marmaduke's and Rufus's brushed and bandaged, were ready to flow magnificently.

Mr White, tall and gaunt and slightly stooping, was my first visitor. He asked if he might borrow our 'Road Closed' jump to keep the visitors' cars out of the Castle.

"I've got better things to do than stand out there all day directing that lot," he complained, as we crossed the paddock.

"His Lordship's convinced that left to themselves they'll be breaking, down the drawbridge. I told him our Amy in the ticket office would soon turn them back, but he won't have it."

"Well this should do the trick," I said picking up the plank part of the jump and leaving him to carry the posts.

"If they can read," said Mr White contemptuously.

As we walked back, remembering that Lisa had said he was the only competent male in the Castle, I asked how I could get a new broomhead. "Mr Sterne said he would do something, but nothing's happened," I grumbled in my turn.

"Leave it with me," said Mr White. "I'm not promising mind, but I'll see what can be done."

"And you couldn't lend me a pair of clippers, could you?" I asked, sensing an ally. "I want to cut back those creepers that have grown over the loosebox windows."

Mr White said that he would see what he could do and, when we had erected the 'Road Closed', I left him smiling sardonically as he watched the visitors turn obediently into the park.

Chris arrived next. He seemed nervous and quite reproachful when he found that Charlie and I had already cleaned the tack.

"Well if you don't need any help, I might give Rufus a quiet school in the lists," he said. "Ride him round the tilt, keeping him on the bit, and try to persuade him that there's nothing to get het up about; what do you think?"

"Good idea," I agreed. "In fact the more you tire him out the better. I'd take him for a hack too."

"We don't want the poor old lad on his knees," objected Chris.

"If there's nothing to hold back, you'll *have* to ride forward," I pointed out, "and at least he won't be stargazing.

By the way, I found some leather roundings in Great Aunt Hermione's chest. You know, those little straps, which buckle on to pelhams, "I added when Chris looked at me blankly. "They enable children with small hands to ride with one rein. I thought you'd better use them this afternoon."

Chris stretched out a large hand and observed it ruefully.

"I'd never thought of myself as having small ones, but if you say so. . ."

I giggled. "You know perfectly well what I mean. You have to ride one-handed because of the lances and spears. Two reins add to your problems and knotting the lower one looks messy."

"You're right. I was planning to take off the lower one, but this device for tiny hands sounds a better bet. Keep it under your hat though. I can just hear the cracks about my tiny hands being frozen from Mark."

As Chris set off on Rufus Mr Sterne and Walter Melville appeared. They were laden with eight bright yellow banners and called to me to help them to load the Range Rover.

Mr Melville was in a great state of agitation and every time he tried to tick off his action list, his clipboard was missing.

"White has done the flags. I've attached the decorative shields to the tilt," he announced, ticking wildly when I had retrieved the clipboard from under the sack of heads. "Now Laurence, you've taken up the table, table cloth, chairs and P.A. .?"

"I took up a load of stuff, not sure what was in it. Felicity and White said it was everything you wanted," Mr Sterne answered vaguely.

"Well we'd better get up there and check it," said Mr Melville, tutting impatiently.

When Chris returned he said that Rufus had gone better than he expected, but that Walter was flapping and wanted him up at the lists. I took Rufus and sponged out his saddlemark and brushed over the rest of him. Then I fed all three horses, and deciding to take advantage of a lull, went off to have an early lunch myself.

The lull didn't last long. First a bearded knight of Lyme appeared to ask if it was O.K. to take down the 'Road Closed' as they had been told to park by the garages and then Felicity and Ben banged on the cottage door and handed me a carrier bag containing my fancy dress.

"We hope it fits," said Felicity. "Mum asked Lisa about your size and she said it would."

"Hundreds of people have come to see the Castle," Ben told me.

"Many more than Mum expected. Some of them are having lunch in the tea room and staying to see the jousting."

"They're spending masses in the shop," Felicity added gloatingly. "Michelle says she's been rushed off her feet. I helped her for a bit."

When the Sternes had gone, I changed into my outfit: slim-legged, black velvet trousers and a red satin shirt, gold braided and loose enough to pass as a tabard. There were no shoes, so I tried on my riding boots, but they looked too modern and clumsy. However my ordinary winter boots went quite well, especially when I turned the tops down.

I had eaten lunch and was trying the effect of a belt over the tabard, when there was another bang on the door and Charlie burst in.

"What do you think of this?" he asked indignantly. "I'm supposed to be a page or a herald. I think it's too· tight and really yuk," he went on, pirouetting for my inspection," but Mum says it's O.K. and I've got to wear it."

He was too squarely built to look right in black velvet knee breeches, worn with white stockings and buckled shoes, and his square, pink and white face and thick lensed glasses did look rather ridiculous sandwiched between a frilled white shirt and a flat-topped velvet hat with a curling plume.

"We've got to look a bit silly. But it's in a good cause," I reminded him.

"You don't look silly," said Charlie inspecting me. "In fact you look nicer than you do in jeans. It's my specs that really ruin everything," he went on despondently. "*And* I've been given a bugle which I can't blow. Dad says it doesn't matter and I'm just to go through the motions when the canned music comes on."

"Cheer up, count your blessings," I told him. "At least you haven't got to joust in front of a huge crowd on Rufus, like poor old Chris."

We found Felicity and Ben, dressed in knee breeches and purple shirts, parading round the yard, their yellow banners held high, while the geldings gazed at them in amazement and Fiesta issued piercing snorts.

"Our shoes don't fit," Felicity told me cheerfully. "They were made for Dad and the aunts when they were young. Mine are too pointed and they pinch."

"Mine fall off when I run," grumbled Ben, "but Mum says I've got to grin and bear it." He grinned horribly, pulling his lips wide with his fingers. "Can I have another go on the bugle, Charlie? I want to practise rude noises."

Suddenly the yard was full of people and they all seemed to be demanding my help. The Lyme knights had left their hoof oil behind, Mr Melville had lost his gauntlets, Chris was calling for help with caparisoning an already het-up Rufus, and Mark was enquiring if I had a sewing kit, as he had split a seam in his tabard. I sent Ben as custodian of the hoof oil, with strict instructions to see that it came back. I asked Felicity to hold Rufus and, when I had found Mr Melville's gauntlets in Marmaduke's manger. I dashed to the cottage for a safety pin. Mark was obviously disatisfied with my rough and ready repair, but I pointed out that we had to assemble in nine minutes, there was no time to sew.

Eventually they were all ready and, as the Knights of Lyme rode into the yard our knights led out their horses and mounted.

I felt proud of my charges. They looked magnificent in their caparisons and they were showing off outrageously. Fiesta was prancing, Marmaduke champing and pawing and Rufus, arching his neck and overbending, at least looked much more like a warhorse that when he stargazed.

We formed up: Ben and Charlie, Felicity and I ahead of the Lyme foot people; a marshal, six men-at-arms, rough and brawny in leather jerkins, and two ladies in long, medieval dresses, who were to keep the scores.

The Knights of Lyme were directed to hold back and give the walkers a start, and the Knights of Sterne were told to bring up the rear.

It seemed a long way up the park to the lists and I felt slightly self-conscious in my fancy dress, especially as the spectators were still arriving and some of them walked up beside us making remarks and staring. Felicity and Ben didn't mind. Felicity was muttering uncomplimentary remarks about them and Ben was clowning with the bugle. But I could see that Charlie was suffering. He kept looking back as though to make sure that we hadn't deserted him and his face was scarlet with either heat or embarrassment.

We reached the pavilion and, as the medieval ladies seated themselves at the table, the knights lined up facing them and the rest of us sloped off to our lance racks.

Then, as the knights galloped round the tilt in turn, Mr Sterne read out their biographies and the spectators applauded. Watching, I was impressed, both with Lyme and Sterne. It was hard to believe that those tall and awe-inspiring figures in their crested and feathered helms were really ordinary modern men and included Chris and Mr Melville.

As soon as the introductions were over, four men-at-arms opened the proceedings with a single-stick fight at either end of the tilt, and our knights joined us at the lance rack.

"Here, take this accursed thing," called Chris, tearing

off his helm. "It's giving me claustrophobia. Can you see anything in yours, Mark?"

"Not much, but one learns to accept its limitations," answered Mark, tightening Fiesta's girth.

"I don't," grumbled Chris. He and Mr Melville were pulling on their kamals, the imitation chainmail balaclavas with cowls attached, which made them look low-browed and distinctly sinister.

Mark was riding bareheaded as usual. He and Fiesta made a stunningly handsome pair. A true Sir Lancelot, I thought, trying to remember *Morte D'Arthur*. Hadn't he been the hero of Camelot until he fell in love with the Queen?"

Then Chris called me to check his stirrup leathers.

"They're in the usual holes, I've counted twice, but the left one feels much longer than the right. Do you think they've been mixed up with Mark's or Walter's?"

"No," I answered inspecting the second one. "They're a pair and they're yours. "Mark's are newer and Mr Melville's wider. It's nerves; it happens to everyone at shows and gymkhanas."

"Kate," Felicity was calling me, "We've got to do the rings."

The purple knight of Lyme opened the tournament proper. He thundered down one side of the tilt, speared a collection of rings from the quintain post with unerring aim, and made another successful raid on the second post. Replenishing my quintain I found he had carried five rings and Felicity called that all six had gone from her side. We sent Charlie and Ben to retrieve them as Mr Melville set off.

Marmaduke thundered even more impressively than the Lyme horse and Mr Melville returned waving his lance and shouting, "Ten!"

"Eleven," argued Felicity looking at the solitary ring left on her post.

"Dropped one," he sounded out of breath. "You'll find it over there."

Lyme's yellow knight also did well and was loudly clapped. The spectators seemed to be warming up. Then it was Mark. He and Fiesta sped round, looking brilliant as well as beautiful and, when their maximum score of twelve was announced, there was tremendous applause. Rushing to congratulate Mark and pat Fiesta, I failed to see the third Lyme knight, but Ben told me, with undisguised delight, that he had missed my post altogether and carried only five of Felicity's rings.

Then Chris, who has been circling feverishly, started slowly, lost control and, with Rufus swerving about, managed to miss both posts. The Sterne children groaned, but their father, with unscripted tact, told the audience that the last two knights were young and they and their horses were still undergoing training.

We cleared the rings away, as I set up my quintain, there were frantic calls from Felicity who couldn't make hers slot over its post. I ran to help and as we struggled with it a voice said, "Don't panic," and a tall man with an outsize nose and tightly curled reddish hair, came to our rescue. When I thanked him he said, "You're welcome. Name's Trevor Fletcher; I'm joining the Sterne lot." There was no time for conversation, so I shouted, "Great," as I fled back across the tilt to square my own quintain for the first of the Lyme knights.

Lyme were good. As they hurtled round, one behind the other, I was too busy grabbing the swinging counterweight and straightening the shield, to keep their score, but the rapid succession of galloping horses and the constant bangs as the lances struck, made a thrilling spectacle and the audience applauded enthusiastically.

I was afraid that, in comparison, our knights would appear amateurish, but they got going too. Mr Melville, grimly purposeful, only missed once. Mark, riding superbly, made all of his six strikes seem easy, and Chris, though he missed three times, was using his legs, riding forward, and managing to look quite knight-like as he chased the others round the tilt.

As Mr Sterne announced a ten minute interval, during which liquid refreshment would be available, I hurried to the lance rack to congratulate our riders.

"Weren't they good?" I said to Charlie who appeared beside me.

"Better than I expected," he admitted grudgingly, "but we're trailing as far as points go. The scoring's complicated. Ben and I have been talking to the mediaeval ladies. They say the rings have the least value, one point, because there are more of them. You get two for striking the quintain, three for spearing a head and four for a strike in the joust and there's a maximum of twelve points for each section."

"You were great," I told Mark, who was loosening Fiesta's girth.

"Thanks." He handed me her reins. "I'm panting for some of this 'liquid refreshment'."

"I'm panting for some more scores," announced Ben, waving his notebook. "I make us two behind in the quintain and four in the rings, which isn't too bad."

"Don't get too hopeful. The worst is yet to come, for me anyway," Chris told him.

"Mark hasn't dropped a point," said Felicity tactlessly. "He's been fantastic so far."

"If you're holding Fiesta you may as well hold Rufus and I'll get us *both* a drink," Chris told me, casting an angry glance at the trestle table from which a Lyme supporter was selling the drinks. "Coke do?"

"Fine thanks," I answered and looking across I saw that Mark, coke in hand, had joined the Lyme knights.

At the end of the interval Mr Sterne announced the scores. Ben was right, Lyme had only fifty-six to our fifty. As the spectators clapped Charlie and I looked at each other.

"You can't call that trailing," I told him. "We're giving them a good match, in fact it's terrific for our first time."

I didn't see much of the sword fight, as I was straightening caparisons and handing out spears, but it looked more exciting than the single-stick battles. The moment it ended the Sternes and I hurried in to scatter the heads, while Mr Sterne read out his piece on the Infidels playing football with Christian heads and the Crusaders retaliating with spearing practice. But they had become the 'so-called' Infidels and he had added a bit of his own on the disgracefulness of the Crusades. I looked round to see if Mr Melville was tutting with annoyance at his script being changed, but as he was cantering round making spearing gestures he probably hadn't heard.

The purple knight again rode first for Lyme.

"He's their organiser," said Mark as I passed him on the way out of the tilt. "He seems a sensible bloke; I've got him to agree to a number of improvements for our next meeting."

"He's good at this too," I answered as we watched him make a vicious stab at his first head. Then, with it impaled firmly on his spear, the purple knight gave a triumphant war whoop and galloped for our end. I pulled the head off for him and he raced away down the other side of the tilt, spearing another and then, making it look easy, a third. But, perhaps through over confidence, he missed his fourth.

One of the Lyme red knights came next. They both wore scarlet, a colour which hadn't the dignity of Mr Melville's deep crimson.

"They're brothers," Mark told me. "This is the younger one and, as we can only field three men, he's doing the rings and heads and his brother the quintain and the joust."

The younger brother speared two heads, missed the third and then failed to carry the fourth for four lengths so it didn't count. To the delight of the Sterne camp the yellow knight also missed one.

"Great, they only got twenty-four for that round— now we'll show them," Ben announced loudly.

"That doesn't sound very chivalrous," Chris told him. "And don't start crowing yet, there's still plenty of opportunity for me to mess thing up."

But when Mr Melville carried all four head our spirits rose uncontrollably. We were only six points behind— we might even win—but then, unbelievably, Mark missed. We groaned and the crowd groaned with us, but I could see some unchivalrous glee at the other end of the tilt. However, Mark had learned his lesson and speared his next three heads with careful skill.

"We're only three points behind in this one and nine in the whole thing," announced Charlie after an inspection of Ben's notebook. "But now it's Chris."

The suspense was too much for all of us. Charlie and Felicity clung on to my arms and, after Chris missed his first head, they covered their eyes and their hands and refused to watch. But then he suddenly became aggressive and jabbed the second one with unusual ferocity. Then to our delight he carried a third and then, incredibly, a fourth.

We were all shouting, "Brilliant!" "Terrific!" "Well done!" when Chris galloped in. He gave me his spear and began to pat Rufus excitedly.

"We're equal, we're equal," Ben shouted, while Mr Melville filled with justified pride, began to talk of the next joust.

"We're going to put young Trevor into training so if you could get your friend Adrian along, we'd have the foundation of a very strong team," I heard him telling Mark. "Do you think he's serious about joining?"

Mark shrugged, "I've made the best case I can, but I've a feeling he's going to settle for the boat. I can see his point: lower upkeep, no winter feeding and you can take your girlfriend along."

"Kate, we need you," Felicity's voice called indignantly.

"We've got to clear up the heads."

As we collected the scattered heads we listened to Mr Sterne explaining that in medieval times regular tournaments were essential for knights to practise the use of arms, but that the single combat of the joust, when two riders crashed together at a combined speed of over forty miles per hour proved too dangerous, even though the lances were blunted. In the fourteenth century three members of the noble house of Salisbury had died while jousting, one killed by his own son, and many other knights had suffered death or serious injury. But it was only after the death of King Henry II of France in 1559 that the true joust had been abandoned and tilting, with the fence between the contestants, had been introduced instead.

As we carried our sacks of heads back to the lance rack, Mr Sterne went on to explain that each of the three Knights of Sterne would ride against each of the three Knights of Lyme. That they would earn four points for a strike on their opponent's shield, but to strike the horse, or the man, elsewhere than on his shield, would entail disqualification.

Mr Melville and the high-crested purple knight were called first. Wearing their helms, carrying their shields and heavy lances, they had again become faceless and formidable strangers. They trotted down the tilt, met, and in a courtly manner turned to bow to the ladies in the pavilion, then they rode back to their own ends and took up their positions.

When the Lyme Marshal gave the command it seemed nerve-rackingly real. We watched the two stout horses thundering down on each other, the riders holding them close to the tilt and aiming their awesome lances across it. There was a clash, and both riders swayed in their saddles. Mr Sterne, sounding excited, announced a double strike. The spectators cheered.

"Four each," said Ben, opening his notebook.

I congratulated Mr Melville as I took his lance, shield and helm, but I was watching Mark. he was to ride against the elder of the red knights. Fiesta was loving every moment of her salute and showing off to the crowd, but the red knight's horse looked unhappy and, when the command to charge came, he napped and resisted his rider. The Lyme people got him going with arm-waving and shooing, but the disorganized red knight missed, while Mark, unruffled by the delay, made a perfect strike.

"Don't faint, we're in the lead," Ben told me.

"Not for long," said Felicity. "Chris will lose."

Mark asked me to straighten Fiesta's horsecloth so I didn't see Chris's ride, but I knew from the Sterne groans that he had missed.

"Sorry folks," he said when came cantering back. "I couldn't get my lance lined up and I didn't dare risk jabbing him in the stomach."

"Quite right," said Mr Melville, disappearing into his helm.

"Since we were in the lead I'd have thought it was just the moment *to* take a calculated risk," snapped Mark and suddenly I could see that he really cared about winning.

"Sorry." said Chris again, as we all turned to watch the red knight. He seemed to have his horse under better control this time and a row of Lyme people were brandishing spears behind him. Mr Melville was going well and to the crowd's delight, there was another double strike.

Then it was Mark's turn and, to our consternation, Fiesta became over-excited. She gave a large buck and then raced down the tilt at such a speed that Mark and the yellow knight both missed. The crowd loved it, but Mark became stern and silent. He grew even more remote when Chris lost against the purple knight, who, plainly in tremendous form, landed him a really hefty blow.

"They've gone ahead again," Ben told me gloomily as Mr Melville and the yellow knight faced each other. Their horses were swerving a little as they set off down the tilt and I wondered if the men were beginning to tire under the weight of the heavy lances. In a bad position, Mr Melville didn't attempt a strike, but the yellow knight, jabbing recklessly across the barrier, struck him mid-shield, instead of on the outside corner, and caused him to lurch in his saddle. Mr Melville regain his seat and cantered on, but the yellow knight dropped his lance and rode past us, clutching his wrist and cursing.

Then there was a delay while several Lyme knights, a local doctor, a watching nurse, Trevor Fletcher and Ben, inspected the wrist.

Mark seized the opportunity to abandon his lance and school Fiesta, making her halt from the the trot and canter, demanding total obedience. I talked to Chris, guessing that the wait was making him nervous, for he had none of Mark's icy, rather frightening, calm.

"It's worse for the red knight on that nappy animal," I told him. "He must be wondering if he'll start at all."

"I think the Lyme contingent are arming themselves to make certain he does," answered Chris, "I only hope they drive him up his own side of the tilt, I don't want to face sudden death in full frontal combat like the Salisburys."

At last the wrist inspectors moved out of the tilt and

Mr Sterne announced that the programme would continue.

"Good luck," I called to Mark, for this ride, against the purple knight, would be his toughest so far.

Fiesta was subdued and on her best behaviour as the two men, savagely intent, swept towards each other. They met with another of these fearful full speed clashes; it was a double strike. As the spectactors applauded Chris rode a hasty circle and I watched the red knight being led to the tilt through a forest of intimidating spears.

"Best of luck," I called to Chris. if only he could land *one* strike, I thought. He'd done so well in all the other events, one strike in the joust would make his day.

The red knight started. Rufus was going forward, straight and well-positioned, close to the tilt. As the knights approached each other I concentrated, willing Chris to strike. Come on Chris, come on, I willed and suddenly it happened. A single clash; he had struck and the red knight had missed.

A great cheer went up for the Sterne camp, mostly for Chris, but partly because we'd done much better than we expected and losing by a few points was an honourable defeat.

"I make it four points, not bad for our first go," said Ben. "And those four points were for the mis–strike by the yellow knight," added Charlie. "The medieval ladies weren't sure what to do about it. Dad told them to give the points to the Lymes."

"I wondered where you had disappeared to," I told Charlie as we watched the knights lining up in front of the pavilion and listened to the official score: one hundred to Sterne, one hundred and four to Lyme.

"Well you didn't need me after the heads so I helped with the scoring," explained Charlie. "The medieval ladies are quite agreeable, but they're useless with figures and they waste a lot of time arguing. I told Dad that we need a laptop computer, then we could give the updates in seconds; it would make the whole thing much more exciting."

"What did he say?" I asked.

"Nothing much, he sort of grunted. Listen to that," Charlie went on indignantly. "He's let the Lyme Marshal take over the mike."

I listened. As the knights galloped a final lap of honour a very different voice from Mr Sterne's told the spectators to give them all, winners and losers, a big hand. "Come again soon and be sure and tell your friends about the magnificent spectacle you've seen today," it exhorted. "Now drive home carefully, and *take care.*

"Dad would have done better than that. I don't know why he lets people push him around," grumbled Charlie.

"I think you're rather like him, nice, but not forceful. Perhaps you *both* need assertion training," I suggested with a laugh.

Our knights handed us their lances and shields and rode off towards the stables, chatting happily with the Knights of Lyme. The Sternes and I found ourselves left with the clearing up. We stored the various tables and chairs and Mr Melville's precious wooden shields, which had decorated the tilt, in the pavilion. We collected the abandoned coke cans and, when we had loaded the Range Rover with the public address system and the rubbish sacks as well as the knightly gear, there was no room for passengers, so the children and I followed it down the park, grumbling about our weary legs. As we unloaded spears and lances I could hear voices across the yard and I began to hope that the knights were cleaning their tack. But when having said goodnight to the Sternes and collected Fiesta's saddle from her door, I made for the tackroom. I was amazed to find a party in full swing.

"Oh good, here's Kate at last." Lisa seemed to be the hostess, presiding over the cottage kettle, teabags and mugs and an enormous chocolate cake. "Where have you been?"

"Clearing up of course," I answered looking round at the munching knights. "We've put your gear away." I added reproachfully.

Chris began to apologise, but Mr Melville interrupted him.

"We've given the horses their haynets," he said virtuously.

"What Kate needs is some tea," Mark told Lisa. She pored me a mug and cut me a huge slice of cake.

"Weren't they marvellous?" she asked. "I was so impressed I thought we *had* to celebrate."

"Terrific," I agreed, accepting the stool that Chris was offering.

Lisa turned back to Mark. They were both sitting on Great Aunt Hermione's chests. "Do go on with your story, it's absolutely hilarious."

Having missed the beginning, the story didn't seem particularly funny to me, so, when I had eaten my cake and gulped down my tea, I told them, "I'm going to change and then do the horses."

"Right," said Chris. "We'll discard our knightly gear

and join you."

"Yes, duty calls," Mr Melville got up stiffly and bowed to Lisa. "Thank you for the tea."

"Be with you in a minute," Mark called after us.

When I returned, Mr Melville was rubbing down Marmaduke, Chris was filling water buckets and the sound of animated conversation was still coming from the tackroom. I brushed Fiesta over, topped up her water bucket, and was retrieving her caparisons from the manger, when Chris looked in and asked if we were ready to feed.

"Just about," I answered. "I've done Fiesta."

"That lazy so-and-so Mark is supposed to do his own horse on jousting weekends," said Chris indignantly. "You mustn't let us exploit you, Kate."

"I'll have to work something out," I answered vaguely, as I folded Fiesta's caparisons and wondered if *I* needed assertion training.

"Begin as you mean to go on," advised Chris, "that was my Gran's favourite saying."

When we had fed the horses, Chris collected Mr Melville, who was re-organizing the gear store, with many tuts over the way we had mixed lances and spears, and we went back to the tack-room for another go at the tea. Lisa filled our mugs and passed round cake, but she was still monopolising Mark. It wasn't *fair*, I thought childishly. All his attention was focussed on her; it was as though I had ceased to exist.

Chris and Mr Melville sat down on the stools and began to relive every spear stab and lance thrust of the joust. Feeling left out and blaming Lisa for my isolation, for she had taken over my tackroom and my knights, I picked up a bucket and went to fetch warm water from the cottage.

When I came back the atmosphere had changed. Mark greeted me with one of his radiant smiles.

"Oh Kate, I know you think I've been slacking," he said reproachfully," but actually I've been using my administrative abilities on your behalf. Our new knight, young Trevor of the red curls, will deliver four lengths of chain tomorrow at eight-thirty. Four rather than two, because, as he pointed out, it is useless to chain one end of a gate—the yobs, horse thieves or whatever, simply lift it off its hinges. Mr Sterne has promised me that White will produce four large padlocks in the course of the day and I will buzz Trev and the Castle on the car phone to make sure that it all happens." He smiled at Lisa. "So no more sleepless nights."

"Great, a man of action at last. Where have you been all my life?" demanded Lisa flirtatiously.

Trying to hide my jealousy, I said, "Thanks, Mark, I'll sleep a whole lot better knowing that the horses are safe."

There was an awkward silence.

"More cake anyone?" asked Lisa brightly. "This is absolutely your last chance as I must go and finish the Castle dinner. Mercifully it's cold on Sunday nights," she went on, gathering up teabags and the remains of the cake. "Salmon mousse, game pie, rhubarb syllabub and cheese."

Mr Melville smacked his lips. "No chance of an invitation to dinner with the noble Lord?" he asked.

"Not unless you're disguised as a Japanese tourist," Lisa answered. "Now where did I put that surcoat?

"Bye everyone, see you later, Kate," she called, as, laden with kettle and Mark's blue tabard, she made for the cottage.

"What a charmer!" said Mark enthusiastically. "She's not only volunteered to mend my tabard, she's going to embroider it with a gold *fleur-de-lis*, then the populace will know I have royal French blood even when I'm not carrying my shield."

Chris gave me a quick look. "Terrific cake," he said.

"Now, to serious matters." Mr Melville got up as I started to clean Marmaduke's bridle. "You've all met my new recruit. I've asked him over to my place on Monday evening. I thought I could run through the basic terms and gear with him, and I've suggested that he tries the horse out here on Wednesday evening. Are either of you free then?"

"Yes, I can make it," answered Chris. "Does anyone know how much riding he's done? Is he experienced?"

"Showjumping mainly. He says the horse is out of novice classes and not up to the bigger competitions, so he thought he'd try jousting," explained Mr Melville.

Mark was consulting his pocket computer. "I may be tied up on Wednesday—I'll have to let you know."

EIGHT

Lisa had made it clear that though we shared the same day off, we would be spending it separately and, still piqued at the way she had hijacked my tackroom and knights, I had tried to make it equally clear that I, too, would prefer to be on my own. She had friends living on the edge of the New Forest, who were collecting her for lunch and I decided on a visit to Salisbury.

Lisa's hijack had also convinced me that unless I became more travelled, amusing and generally sophisticated I was going to spend the rest of my life losing the Marks of this world to the Lisas of this world, and I had resolved to do something about it.

I knew that I really needed driving lessons, a car and holidays abroad, but since they were all out of reach at present, I decided to start with Salisbury. I would absorb culture by 'doing' the Cathedral and seeing the city. Then I would buy a new dress. Not one of those useful dresses which earn Mum's highest accolade, 'You could wear it anywhere', but a smart and sexy dress which would force Mark to realise, if he ever asked me out again, that I wasn't just a doormat in jeans.

I was up early, since being in sole charge meant that there was no one else to feed and muck out, but Charlie and Felicity had agreed to top up water buckets, and to throw hay to any horse in need at lunchtime.

Trevor appeared punctually at eight-thirty and, finding me in the feedstore, held up fistfuls of long heavy chains.

"Here we go," he said, jangling them triumphantly. "Took a bit of doing to find four."

"Brilliant," I told him, since praise was obviously expected. "They're really thick, no one's going to cut through them."

"Well," he sounded doubtful, "you can cut through anything, but I don't reckon they'll be carrying the right tools. Got the padlocks?"

"No, Mr White hasn't produced them yet."

"Pity, I could have locked the hinges for you. Still, I'll put them in position, then it won't take you a minute when the padlocks come."

"Thank you very much," I called after him as he strode across the yard.

"You're welcome," he shouted back.

I caught the Salisbury bus, it passed through Sterne twice a week, and shared a seat with a succession of elderly ladies. The first one, who was white haired and merry, told me about her daughter and grandchildren in Australia. The second, who was grey haired and gloomy, recounted all the muggings and rapes she had gleaned from her Sunday newspaper. The third the most interesting. She told me the story of the Tolpuddle Mar-

tyrs, the nineteenth century Dorset farm labourers who
had been transported to Australia for seven years because
they started a trade union. But the public protests had
been so great that they were reprieved after two years
and returned as folk heroes.

I was very impressed by the Cathedral, even though
the tallest spire in England was surrounded by scaffold-
ing. I bought a little guide book and walked round
admiring the tombs and effigies. The oldest one
belonged to a Salisbury and was dated 1226, but the
unlucky fourteenth century jousters didn't seem to be
there. I admired the blue stained-glass window, with its
prisoners of conscience theme, and then, deciding that I
didn't have time for any of the museums, walked round
the Cloisters and then the Close.

Afterwards, when I was buying a postcard for Mum in
the shop I met a Japanese girl called Yoshika. She was on
her own because her friend, had stayed behind in the
hotel with a cold, so we had lunch together and she told
me a lot about her family and Japan.

Having written and posted the card to Mum, I went
in search of a dress. As usual I became very depressed as I
trekked round the possible shops, trying on dress after
dress, each of which made me look worse than the last. I
was about to give up when I found one, black and white,
and fashionably short. It made me look different; a bit
older and definitely more interesting. I bought it,
though it took all my spare cash, and comforted myself
with the thought that Mum's emergency fund was there
if needed.

No one talked to me on the journey home, but I
admired the countryside, allowed myself a small fantasy

about going out to dinner with Mark and wondered what Lisa had left in the fridge for supper.

The horses welcomed me with glad, if slightly reproachful neighs and five padlocks awaited me on the tack room table. Four were huge and old, but freshly oiled and in perfect working order, the fifth was smaller, and there was a note from Mr White, explaining that this was for the tackroom door. He had fitted it with a hasp, and he advised me to carry one set of keys 'on my person' and to keep the other set in a safe place in the cottage.

When I had done the horses I padlocked the tackroom and both gates. I was a bit worried about Lisa's reaction to being locked out, but decided that she should be pleased, for the prowlers were at last being taken seriously. Then I hurried to the cottage to inspect my supper: curried chicken and rice, which only needed heating up, and a delicious *crème caramel*.

Two days without riding seemed to have filled the Sternes with new enthusiasm and on Tuesday morning before I had breakfasted I had a visit from Felicity and Ben who wanted to hack in the morning and school with Chris in the evening, and then one from Charlie who wanted to be lunged as well as schooled.

It was quite a rewarding morning. Charlie was beginning to look more at home on Rufus and, as his confidence grew his air of gloom and doom seemed to be lifting. I couldn't make up my mind whether this was because he was now enjoying riding or if it was due to getting so much attention, on a one to one basis, from me.

I began to think about my own childhood. It was true that Mum had worked, but it had mostly been fairly undemanding secretarial work, and all her spare time had been devoted to me. I hadn't had to share her with a father, brother and sister, much less a falling-down castle, a gift shop and flood of tourists.

Perhaps I had been luckier than I realised, but it was impossible to tell what effect siblings might have had on me; they might have made me more enterprising.

Probably it was swings and roundabouts, I told myself, and the only certainty seemed to be that no one got everything.

We had a good hack. I rode Marmaduke and, as Ben and Felicity were both riding with quite respectable forward seats, I made them follow me up and down several gentle slopes. At long last they seemed to have grasped the idea that a horse is controlled with the rider's legs and seat and not with the reins. On the way home they began to compose a rhyme full of the ghastly things that could happen to unwary riders. They argued and giggled so much that most of it was inaudible, but the refrain, which was chanted loudly and clearly went:

'When in trouble, do as Kate begs,
Use your legs. Oh, do use your legs!'

I fitted Fiesta's ride in before lunch and then, afterwards, feeling that I must have a rest before evening stables and schooling, I debated what to do about Tarka. It was obviously ridiculous that I should have to exercise him while the boys spoiled my schooling by sharing Romany. I thought of trying the reproachful angle and telling Charlie that he was far too heavy for poor little

Romany, but decided that he might seize the excuse to give up riding altogether. I wondered if I dared to order Felicity to ride Tarka so that her brother could have Snowy, but supposing she refused? I could suggest to Mrs Sterne that he was sold and replaced by a solid quiet pony, but it seemed short-sighted to part with a pony of Tarka's potential now that the Sternes had started to ride properly.

In the end I decided on a mixture of lungeing and cunning when Felicity and Ben appeared in the yard to tack up their ponies, I was lungeing Tarka close to the yard gate. He had obviously been lunged before, which reinforced my theory that he had been properly broken and schooled and had only acquired bad habits when he found he could bully the Sternes.

"Hi, what about you being lunged?" I called as they stood watching. "It's doing wonders for Chris and Charlie."

"Not on him, *thank you*," answered Felicity. "I wouldn't mind on Snowy."

"Tarka would be much more comfortable," I told her as I called him in and then sent him round the opposite way. "He's young and supple while Snowy's elderly and so a bit stiff. What about you, Ben?"

"Me ride Tarka?" he asked in tones of disbelief.

"Only on the lunge. I'm sure Chris would, but he's so tall."

"O.K., as long as you promise not to let go if he bolts off," Felicity agreed suddenly.

"There's nowhere to bolt to," I pointed out. "And the reins are there for emergencies."

Felicity was soon riding tall and looking really good. I

gave her a lot of praise, but it wasn't really necessary for, now she had realised how it felt to sit correctly, she was trying for her own pleasure and not to oblige me.

Ben was impressed. "She looks different, sort of tall and posh. I think I might like a go after all."

"O.K. in five minutes, but you'll need your hat."

My plan worked brilliantly. When Charlie strolled into the yard Ben had begun to relax and was trying his first trot, but he was still confused about pulling himself down into the deep position.

"Perhaps Charlie would show you," I suggested with low cunning. "He's pretty good at it."

Charlie turned a little pale, but mounted obediently and after his demonstration both Ben and Felicity demanded second turns.

I hate instructing from a horse. You can't let down stirrup leathers, adjust curb chains or shake your fists, but, when Chris arrived and the Sternes were tacked up, I rode Tarka into the school, determined to push on with his rehabilitation.

My chance came quite soon. I was introducing Chris to shoulder-in as a way of getting Rufus back on the bit when he lost him and making the point that it was using your seat and inside leg to activate the horse's inside hindleg that brought his head down, not setting your hands, which was now Chris's worst fault. To Felicity's fury, Snowy, who had obviously never heard of shoulder-in, ignored her aids and stared into space.

"Don't be cross with him," I told her. "He's old and a bit stiff so you can only ask for a very small bend at first. Look, try on Tarka, he's good at it."

She mounted without a word, and finding that she

was doing better than Chris, began to pat Tarka enthusiastically. I told Charlie to get up on Snowy, called Ben from his garden path practice and announced that they would all do leg-yielding. After that I taught them how to make their circles smaller with the outside aids and larger with the inside aids and they all seemed surprised that their hands and legs could act independently and influence their ponies in this indirect way.

It wasn't until I announced that schooling was over and that we would trot over poles and then jump that Felicity tried to seize command.

"Charlie hates jumping, Kate, so I'll have Snowy back. I want to show you how well he jumps; as long as the jumps are not coloured."

Charlie was already dismounting and Chris and Ben were both looking apprehensive and explaining that they had never jumped as high as most of the jumps on Tarka's course.

"Hang on a minute," I had to shout to be heard as I dragged a pole into the centre of the school. "We're not jumping yet, so all stay where you are. Chris, you lead. Round the school and then down the centre and over the pole, keeping at the same steady trot."

Even Rufus managed to stay calm over one pole, but when I added a second he decided that it must be a jump and began to stargaze, so we stood him to one side and let him watch the ponies and, when he had calmed down, we slotted him in behind Snowy, who had a steadying influence. When I added a third pole Tarka and Snowy began to lengthen their strides and swing their backs in the approved manner. Then, while the ponies rested, Chris and I added a tiny jump about three metres from the last of the trotting poles.

"Now sit still and look ahead," I told my pupils. "Keep the ponies going forward, make it all look smooth and easy."

"Supposing they refuse?" asked Felicity.

"Just circle, get your rhythm back and rejoin the ride. And if they canter just bring them gently back to the trot."

The ponies made nothing of the little jump and, the third time round, Rufus calmed down and relaxed.

"Very good, brilliant," I told my pupils, and I rushed round reducing all the oil-drum jumps to one drum high. "Now you do the same thing round the course, just the little jumps. Steady trot, sit still, look ahead and let the ponies carry you over. Three lengths between you and if anything goes wrong, circle."

They set off and I began to shout instructions: Felicity was to sit still, Chris was to circle each time Rufus hotted up. Charlie had forgotten that he was to use his legs *every* stride and Ben must look where he *wanted* to go. I sent them round twice without stopping and then once more on the other rein. When they came back they were all patting their ponies and seemed very pleased with themselves.

"Only Felicity is ready to jump higher today I told them, so while I make a course for her perhaps you can straighten up the bending poles." Chris helped me and Felicity became very bossy, she demanded everything at three quarters of a metre and wouldn't let us include the showjumps.

Then, when she set off, I was horrified by her riding. She seemed to have forgotten everything I had taught her. She didn't circle at the start and she approached each jump with a wild flurry of arms and legs.

"There, you see, he did them all first go," she announced triumphantly as she rode back.

"Without much help from you," I answered sourly. "Can't you understand that a pony needs quiet when he goes into a fence? He has to look at the height and width and choose his take off. How would you like to jump with a maniac on your back who kept pulling at your mouth and kicking you in the ribs?"

"But ponies have to be *made* to jump," she argued.

"No they don't. Once you've got them going well, it becomes a partnership; you've walked the course and they haven't, so all your aids should be signals telling them what sort of fence lies ahead. You can't tell Snowy anything, your aids simply shriek, "Jump! Jump! Jump!" at every fence." Felicity's unresponsive face made it plain that she didn't believe me.

"Here, let me have Snowy, I'll try and show you what I mean." I let down the stirrups and rode round, getting the feel of him. He had a very long slow stride for a pony, a puissance horse rather than a speed merchant, I decided, and a nice ride though a little stiff. I put him over the oil-drum jumps and then, realising that they were far too low for him, went on over the showjumps.

"You're right he is a good jumper," I told Felicity. "He's got tremendous power and yet he's so light on his feet. We'll build him a decent course tomorrow."

Felicity, who seemed a bit subdued, made no objection to bending Tarka and, as we increased the speed by allowing cantering on the way home, it became obvious that Tarka and Romany, with their short strides, were going to be the gymkhana stars.

Later, when we were all cleaning tack at high speed because of the Sterne dinner, Mr Melville appeared.

"Good news," he told us. "The Lyme people were so impressed by the setup here they want to put on a more ambitious tournament on the Sunday after next. I've been having a word with Mr Sterne and he's agreeable provided he's not called upon to give the commentary."

"But that means we'll have that yucky Lyme Marshal all day," protested Ben.

"It's Dad's fault, he's so negative; always opting out of everything," complained Charlie.

"No he's not, he just hates microphones," Felicity argued.

"I gather he has a prior engagement—he's agreed to umpire a cricket match." Mr Melville boomed louder to be heard above the Sterne bickering. "I've told them that there's no hope of our fielding more than four knights and we were discussing the possibility of putting on a junior or novice event to encourage youngsters to take part."

"Great, can I assume novice status?" asked Chris.

"Not unless Lewis makes up his mind to join us," answered Mr Melville. "Young Trevor's a long way behind you at the moment."

On Wednesday morning I was full of energy. I scarcely noticed the mucking out and I sang as I groomed the knights' horses.

I lunged Charlie on Tarka and then, when Felicity appeared and demanded a hack, I told them they could go on their own, as I had no horses needing exercise and

I wanted to smarten up the yard.

They argued. Felicity said I was mean and Ben made his usual protest that it would be no fun without me, and added that the yard already looked a million times smarter than it had when Delia was in charge.

In the end I agreed to go on condition that Felicity rode Tarka, that Charlie came on Snowy, and that they all helped me build a better course of jumps before our next schooling session.

I took Fiesta for the hack and I was very cautious about where we cantered. I didn't want Tarka to lose his reputation as a reformed character. Charlie seemed quite happy on Snowy and helped Ben to invent a new verse of the riding song, which seemed designed to unnerve Felicity:

> 'If your pony bolts off down a precipitous hill
> and you know that you're heading for a horrible spill
> then you must do as Kate always begs,
> Use your legs, oh, do use your legs!

Trevor Fletcher arrived early for the practice and, having inspected the padlocks and chains on both gates, unboxed a dark bay gelding, with lop ears and a wide blaze, whom he introduced lovingly as Fixit. Watching Fixit's enormous hoofs scatter straw round my tidy yard, I suggested that he borrowed Snowy's box.

"'Fraid I haven't managed to get all my gear together yet," Trevor explained apologetically. "But I've written to the address Walter gave me for chain mail and I've given my girlfriend Fixit's measurements; she's going to run up his caparisons, and I'm working on my shield."

"Sounds great," I said, thinking that he and Fixit were

rather alike: the same long face, large ears, enormous hands and feet.

"Walter was in favour of black—'sable', I mean. I wanted something brighter, so we've compromised. I'm going for gold. Or, he calls it. The horse cloth will be black, but with a wide border of gold, and the shield will be gold with a fesse vert, that's a green stripe. Think it'll look O.K.?"

"Brilliant," I assured him, "and you'll be quite different from our lot and the Lyme people."

"Yes, that's what Walter said, but I'm still dubious—maybe I should have held out for purple, that was my first choice."

When Chris arrived I left him to advise on the fesse vert and rushed round, filling up water buckets and haynets.

Mark was late and Mr Melville became very peevish and tutted away, constantly glancing at his watch as he watched me caparisoning Fiesta.

Then Charlie appeared, looking worried. "Message from my father," he told Mr Melville. "He's very sorry but he's still in conference with Mr Akikawa, the Japanese tour organizer, so he can't take the gear up. Can we use one of the other cars?"

"Of course we can't," Mr Melville exploded. "None of us has a hatchback. How can I run this show, when no one else takes it seriously?"

"Sorry, Walter," shouted Mark, vaulting over the yard gate.

"One of our best clients was late for his appointment—nothing I could do." He vanished into the changing loosebox.

"We can carry our own lances up, Kate and Charlie can bring the quintains." Chris began to reorganize.

"Two lances each and spears, then there are the heads," snapped Mr Melville.

"Don't panic, don't panic, I've got the Land Rover," Trevor told him. "I'll unhitch the trailer, won't take a minute. Can you drive, Kate?" he called over his shoulder.

"No," I answered, following to help with the unhitching, "but I am longing to learn."

"Well you ride Fixit up with the others then," said Trevor.

"Charlie and I'll sort this lot out."

We set off on a hack round the park. It was supposed to loosen up the horses and relax the riders, but with Mr Melville lauding Trevor as a loyal and helpful team member and casting baleful looks at Mark, it didn't feel that way.

Mark dropped back and rode beside me.

"Walter's insane," he said in a voice bursting with indignation. "Of course I can't walk out on a client just to be on time for a jousting practice. The stupid prat needs to rethink his priorities."

"I expect it's being semi-retired; he's forgotten what full-time work is like," I suggested soothingly.

"No, he's just obsessive about this jousting, but he must be getting senile if he thinks I'm going to put it before my job," Mark muttered angrily.

Then his mood changed. "Oh well, I mustn't let him spoil my day," he said cheerfully." And the good news is that Lisa's practically finished my tabard. She *is* a clever girl. She's done a magnificent job on it; it's almost a work of art. I'm really touched that she should take so much trouble and I'm rewarding her with dinner at The Stag in Fordingbridge; it's this new place that's had such terrific write-ups."

I was suddenly speechless, mostly with fury at the cool way Lisa had walked off with one of my knights. I knew that I wasn't Mark's type, but even so it was a bitter blow. It's not *fair* I thought as a spasm of jealousy shot through me. It's not fair.

Mark didn't seem to notice my reaction. He was making uncomplimentary remarks about Fixit's appearance and breeding. Then the leading horses began to trot, which gave me the chance to push on and join Chris.

By the time we reached the lists all the lances and spears were neatly arranged on their rack and Charlie was explaining how the quintains fitted on their posts to Trevor. I handed Fixit over and organized the rings, but my mind wasn't on the practice. My anger with Lisa refused to be quelled. She was poaching, I thought indignantly, the knights were mine. I didn't burst into the Castle and chat up her Japanese tourists. She would be furious if I walked into her kitchen uninvited, but that was what she had done to me.

Trevor, whose first attempts were not being very successful, kept coming over to ask my advice and Charlie, longing for approval, constantly pointed out that he was the only Sterne helping me. Felicity and Ben were apparently shirking in front of their grandfather's television.

I was glad when the practice ended. Trevor handed me Fixit's reins, but I didn't want to ride back with Mark.

"Here, you try him," I told Charlie. "He's got a long lolloping stride like Snowy. My hat fits you," I added, plonking it on his head. "Go on, let down the stirrup and get up," I went on as he stood staring at me in amazement. "Chris is waiting for you and I'm going in the Land Rover."

I let the knights settle their horses and busied myself topping up water buckets and mixing feeds. When it seemed that even Mark was going to clean tack, I decided to sweep out Snowy's box, square the muckheap and lay the table for supper.

When they had all gone, only Chris searched me out to say goodbye. I padlocked the yard gates and the tackroom, ignoring the unemptied bucket of dirty water, the lidless tin of saddle soap and the scattered dusters, and retreated to the cottage.

Lisa was punctual and irritatingly cheerful.

"A Mediterranean dinner," she announced. "Pepper soup, stuffed vine leaves with rice and lemon sauce, followed by pears poached in red wine."

"Wonderful," I said trying to sound grateful. She glanced at me sharply.

"Sit down and tuck in, you look exhausted."

"Yes, I am a bit. I did take a rest this afternoon, but perhaps it wasn't long enough."

The soup was reviving and Lisa told me about the Japanese tour organiser's loss of nerve. He had now decided that Japanese dishes must be available as an alternative to the Olde Worlde English food on which he had insisted.

"It's too bad, how *can* I cope with bean curd and seaweed when I'm up to the neck in wild boar, saddle of mutton and junket? It's got to be one or the other and I told him so. But I'm afraid it's goodbye to French cooking as long as they're around. We and the Sternes will have to eat whatever he decides on. Still, at least *I* was sensible and took a decent afternoon break," Lisa went on. "There's this little drying green outside the back door, and I sat there in the sunshine and got on with Mark's tabard. It's almost finished and, when he popped in for a look before the practice, he was over the moon; men really are peacocks."

"So that's why he was late." I tried to subdue the note of jealousy in my voice. "It wasn't a client, he was with you."

Lisa gave me another one of her sharp looks. "You're not being such a ninny as to fall in love with him, are you?" she asked.

"No, of course not." I did my best to sound indignant.

"Good," she handed me a plate of stuffed vine leaves, "because I can't see him having him much time for a cook or a groom. He's one of those guys who can charm the birds off the trees *and* he knows it. The sort who marries the boss's daughter. Still I am getting a dinner out of him and, since he always acts as though he's loaded, I suggested this new place in Fordingbridge. I hear it's wildly expensive, but the food's out of this world."

When I returned from breakfast on Thursday morning I found Charlie waiting in the yard.

"We all want to school at eleven," he said, as he watched me tidying the tackroom, "but if you're going for a hack first I'll come with you."

"Great," I answered. "I've got all three to exercise, no knights until Saturday."

"I'll ride Tarka if you like," Charlie offered. "Provided that you're certain you've cured the bolting off."

"I don't think he'll try it on, but if he does, you sit down, use your legs and put him on a circle until he behaves. I think you could stop him; you've a much stronger seat now."

I rode Marmaduke and kept a sharp eye on Tarka in case he decided to return home to his pony friends, but he looked happy and pleased to be out and, after a rather tense first ten minutes, Charlie became relaxed and talkative.

"There was a major uproar at home this morning," he told me. "Two keys from the board in the dining room passage have gone missing. It's a huge thing with a hook for every key and a label beside it telling which door it belongs to."

"Oh dear, another worry," I said thinking of Mrs Sterne's perpetually harassed expression.

"Yes, my mother thinks a burglary is imminent, because she collected the family silver from the bank yesterday. It's going to be used for the Japanese banquet. Dotty really, because they're having seventeenth century food and all the silver's eighteenth century; it was bought long after the Civil War."

"Have they told the police?" I asked.

"Not yet. You see my father's convinced that the keys are in someone's pocket and he keeps shouting at us all to look. Grandfather's the chief suspect, because he's so vague when it comes to locking things up, and being a bit blind as well he could have taken the wrong ones.

When we returned home we were greeted by Ben and Felicity.

"What's Charlie doing on Tarka?"

"You said you hated him. You told Mum you were never going to ride him again."

"That was before Kate's cure," Charlie answered them. "Did you find the keys?"

"No. We came to tell you about it Kate, but I suppose Charlie's told you already." Ben sounded disappointed.

"Yes, but does anyone know which day they disappeared?" I asked.

"Not exactly, though we're all sure that there were no gaps on the board last week. Mum thinks they were taken by one of the visitors last weekend and now a gang will appear and steal all the Japanese credit cards and travellers' cheques as well as our silver."

"Are the day visitors allowed in that part of the house?" I asked.

"No, but the guides say that sometimes they wander off."

"I do wish we had some *fierce* dogs," Ben looked worried.

"Mumbo and Jumbo are so old they've hardly any teeth and even Becky's going deaf."

"Why not have the locks changed?" I asked, remembering occasions when either Mum or I had lost the flat keys.

"The empty hooks are for the west gate and the armoury," Charlie explained, "but no burglar would want them, so we think he changed the keys around to muddle us. It makes sense."

"And it's very expensive to have locks changed, so we

have to be sure we're changing the right ones." Felicity pointed out.

"It looks as though Dad and Mr White will have to check every key against its lock. That's the only way to find which ones are really missing," added Ben.

"But it's going to take hours and as Dad's still convinced they're in someone's pocket, he's not keen to start," observed Charlie with a critical edge to his voice.

"I think it's Mr Melville," said Felicity. "He's only supposed to use the library, but Lisa says she found him wandering about by the dining room on Tuesday and, when she asked if she could help him, he *said* he was looking for Dad."

"And he's the only person who would want such peculiar keys," agreed Charlie.

"I'd rather it was him than a gang of burglars," observed Ben with a shudder.

"But Tuesday *was* the day he talked to your father about the Grand Tournament, wasn't it?" I asked, thinking back.

"You're as bad as Dad, Kate," Felicity scolded. "Just because he was a solicitor you think he couldn't break the law or do anything mean. It's just not true, the papers often have bits about crooked lawyers."

"So do the classics, Dickens and Co. are full of them," Charlie backed her up.

"It's Mr Melville I don't see as a villain, not solicitors in general," I protested.

Our schooling was very successful. Charlie rode Tarka throughout and though he seemed anxious when it came to jumping, he negotiated a small course at the trot very efficiently. I controlled myself and didn't say "I told you so" when Felicity, riding properly, flew over the three show jumps with no trouble at all. Ben fell off when Romany, confused about which jump she was supposed to be heading for, ran out. But he wasn't hurt and it at last made him listen to my cries about looking at the jump ahead and not the one you were jumping.

When I locked up that night I wished that I had asked for padlocks and chains for the paddock gate into the west drive. If it was really the key to the west drive that was missing, the horse thieves might be planning to park their cattle truck by that gate—which, unlike the village entrance, was in a lonely road and far from any houses— and lead the horses across the paddock and down the drive to it. The ponies weren't as valuable as the horses, but I imagined the thieves, balked of their main prey, taking them instead.

I worried about it all evening and it was only as we were going to bed that I decided to act.

"Where's the torch?" I asked Lisa. "I'm worried about the ponies, so I'm going to move the chains from the yard paddock gates to the west drive one. Because if the horse thieves can't into the paddock, they can't get into the yard either."

"It's beside my bed," Lisa answered. "I thought it wasn't much use to you as you never hear anything."

When I had collected the torch and the keys from the pocket of my dirty jeans, I was surprised to find Lisa waiting at the door wearing a jacket.

"I'm coming with you," she said. "You'll need some-one to hold the torch and I don't fancy staying here on my own. Hang on while I lock the door."

"But we're only going across the paddock—it won't take us five minutes," I protested.

"Quite, and we don't want to find someone in the cottage when we get back," she snapped as she tested the door to make sure it was locked, and pocketed the key.

"You don't think it's Mr Melville then?" I asked as I unchained the gate. "Felicity said that you caught him snooping in the passage near the keyboard."

"No, I think he's a nosy old boy who loves people with titles, but I can't see him as a cat burglar or a horse thief. Besides, there were two of them. At least two of them. Unless it was a madman talking to himself."

"Perhaps Trevor Fletcher is Mr Melville's accomplice," I suggested, trying to lighten the atmosphere.

"What's that?" Lisa switched off the torch and clutched my arm. I stared into the darkness.

"Oh, it's all right, it's Tarka," I told her.

"Are you sure?"

"Yes, that noise is grazing. Look, there are the other two." I pointed. Snowy and the white parts of Romany glimmered in a ghostly fashion, but Tarka's unrelieved brown made him invisible.

Lisa's jumpiness was infectious and by the time we reached the far gate I was looking over my shoulder and expecting horse thieves to come creeping down the drive. My hands shook so much that I dropped one of the keys and it took us ages to find it in the grass. We were both very relieved to get back to the cottage, but, even though the door was locked, Lisa insisted on searching for prowlers and only relaxed when she had convinced herself that there was no one under our beds or lurking in the shower.

NINE

I had expected that a weekend without a joust would be a peaceful one, but Chris, Charlie and now Felicity all demanded to be lunged as well as schooled and Trevor appeared for endless unofficial practices in the lists. It was true that Trevor brought his own helpers to carry gear and work the quintain, but since they were either girl friends or younger brothers, who knew nothing about jousting, they pursued me everywhere asking for help and advice.

I introduced grid jumping on Friday evening and the sight of four poles with only a bounce stride between each of them, caused such an outcry from the Sternes and Chris, who'd turned up unexpectedly, that I had to borrow Tarka and then Snowy to prove it could be done. When after a lot of Klaus-style shouting I managed to convince them that maintaining impulsion and looking at the last jump was all the rider had to do, they began to whiz over in fine style, though Ben was still taking a firm hold of Romany's mane.

Charlie was looking so much more confident that I let

146

him jump the show jumps at their lowest height, but Rufus was still hotting up, so Chris had to share Romany's course and circle at the trot between the fences.

On Saturday there was a general jousting practice and Mark arrived early, obviously by arrangement with Lisa, for she appeared at once and announced loudly that he'd come for a fitting of his tabard and perhaps a coffee. Then, both laughing and with Mark bending down a little so that he wouldn't miss a word of her witty chatter, they went off to the Castle.

Feeling rejected I oiled hoofs and then, with a sudden spurt of anger, I decided to be a doormat no longer. Mark could tack up his own horse. I gave Mr Melville a brisk "Good morning", waved at Chris and went to help Trevor, who was loading his Land Rover with lances.

Mark reappeared as I was climbing on Fixit, and Trevor was promising to teach me to drive.

"You won't even need a provisional licence," he was telling me. "So long as we stay on the Sterne land."

I watched Mark glance over Fiesta's door and then shoot me a reproachful look as he hurried for his tack, and I was spitefully glad when Mr Melville on a restive Marmaduke, pursued him across the yard complaining of his bad time-keeping and lack of team spirit.

At the lists I handed over Fixit and sent Trevor to join the other knights in their hack round the park, while I unloaded lances and set up the rings. I was beginning to wonder how on earth we could manage without the Sternes, when Charlie arrived.

"Sorry, Kate," He looked flushed with heat and hurrying.

"We've had another major uproar over those missing keys. Dad's gone through all Grandfather's pockets and his own *and* turned out both Mum's bags without finding them, so this morning he insisted on a complete search of the Castle, every room, every table, bookshelf, window ledge, chimney piece; it's taken hours."

"And you didn't find them?"

"No, but the others are still searching. I only got away by reminding Dad that you couldn't possibly work two quintains at once."

"What's going to happen if they're not found?"

Charlie shrugged. "Dad's checked some of the keys and Mum's trying to hurry him up. She want the locks changed quickly—she says if the Japanese are robbed we'll never get another tour and all the capital expenditure will be down the drain. But Dad's dragging his feet, he's still convinced that they're lying around somewhere and. . ."

The return of the knights interrupted him.

"We've decided to change the order of events." Mr Melville made the decision sound momentous. "We will now quintain first, lance the rings second, spear the heads third and joust last as usual."

"Quintain, rings, heads," I repeated. "And is this just for to day? What about Sunday?"

"Both, it's a permanent change, subject to Lyme confirmation of course, but Mark's already mooted it to Frank Grigson and got his provisional approval."

It was an uneventful practice, except that Rufus went much better than usual and Trevor, who seemed to have taken on Chris's role of clown, hardly scored a point.

Afterwards Charlie climbed up on Fixit without being

told and Trevor insisted on giving me my first driving lesson. It was a stationary lesson on what everything was called and how most of it worked. I was really longing to get down to the stables and settle the horses, but, guessing that Trevor's ego had been bruised by his poor performance in the lists, I put on an attentive air and tried to be intelligent about the workings of gearboxes and chokes.

"Why didn't I think of teaching you to drive?" asked Chris when the others had all gone and we were mixing feeds. "It would be a small return for all you've done for me and Rufus. He really is a changed horse: far easier to ride and as Walter pointed out he *looks* different, his neck muscles have begun to develop, and he'll soon have a crest. You're a miracle worker."

"No, it was just the application of sound principles of equitation," I told him, "but thanks all the same."

"And I've had a brilliant idea." Chris looked pleased. I'll let Trevor teach you the elementary stuff and, when you get your provisional licence, I'll take you out on the roads and instruct you in the dressage of driving."

"That's a promise," I told him. "Nothing like having two cars to dent."

Lisa was in cheerful mood and didn't mention either Mark or the lost keys as we dined on *consommé* soup, *fricasseé* of rabbit, with bacon rolls, *croûtons*, rice and a salad followed by a delicious gooseberry fool.

"The Japs ate theirs like lambs," she told me, "though I did relent and put on a couple of extra fish dishes. Anyway, so far no complaints and they've settled in without any major dramas." She sounded pleased. "Apparently they're very impressed by the size of the rooms and

absolutely amazed by the four-poster beds. I suppose, if
you're used to futons, they do seem a bit over the top.
Now I'm absolutely knackered, so if you don't mind,
when I've locked up I'll leave you to do the dishes and
go to bed.

On Sunday morning the three Sternes appeared in the
yard together and approached me in the solemn manner
of a delegation.

"Kate." As usual Felicity spoke for them. "We're a bit
bored with the knights' procession, you know, when we
walk up to the lists, and we thought it would look more
impressive for this grand tournament if we rode the
ponies. Mum's quite in favour, but she said to ask you."

"Well it's really up to Mr Melville," I answered as I
considered the implications. "But it would mean extra
tack cleaning and grooming. Snowy and Romany would
both need washing and I would be too busy with the
knights' horses to help. Are you sure you wouldn't find
the extra work even more boring?"

"If they had caparisons we'd only have to wash tails
and oil hoofs," suggested Ben with a grin.

"Only warhorses are caparisoned, we'd have saddle
cloths and they don't hide anything." Felicity spoke
severely.

"I think Mr Melville would be pleased. He's always
going on about getting youngsters in and having a
novice event," Charlie reminded me. "I know we're not
good enough for that yet, but processing would get the
ponies used to the crowds."

"Yes, you're right about that," I agreed. "Well if Mr
Melville gives it the O.K. and you'll both help Ben wash

Romany, I'm for it; I think it's a great idea."

"I'll ring Mr Melville then," said Felicity. "It's no use waiting for Mum and Dad to get around to it. And we've got to find saddle cloths."

"And think of some way of disguising hard hats," added Charlie.

"The knights don't wear them," grumbled Ben.

"No, but Mum says we've got to. I think the velvet hats might stretch over them, I'm going to experiment," said Charlie.

Chris had arranged to borrow Fiesta for the Sunday schooling, so I was able to use him to demonstrate sitting deep during transitions to the elder Sternes and to teach him the beginnings of the half halt, which could be useful in jousting.

When it came to jumping, Fiesta was appalled by the striped canvas of some old deck chairs, which I had found in the barn and used to fill in under the pole and drum jumps. Having shied and snorted and gazed at them with goggling eyes, she jumped them with enormous leaps, which left Chris stirrupless or hanging round her neck in undignified positions.

Tarka and Snowy, to the great delight of their owners, made no fuss at all, and both jumped neat clear rounds.

The Sterne bending was also improving and even Ben was beginning to ride quite fast, so I introduced the stone and bucket race, the stones standing in for potatoes, and insisted that they all rode with one hand.

As I held the stones and shouted at the Sternes not to throw but to halt, ride round the bucket, and *drop* the stone in, I decided that my next introduction would be flag races and, by carrying stouter and stouter flags, we would get the ponies used to the idea of spears and lances.

My day off came round again. Since Mark seemed to have attached himself to Lisa and there was no longer any hurry about my becoming sophisticated and cultured, I decided on a restful day at the cottage. But as there was housework—Lisa said it was my turn—washing all those filthy jeans and no laundrette in the village, and a long letter from Mum to be answered, it turned out to be less restful than I had hoped.

It was lunchtime before I got to Mum's letter and I could tell that my postcard from Salisbury, which had mentioned the buying of a new dress and going out, for a drink with Mark had set the alarm bells ringing. For, sandwiched between her accounts of Robbie's teething and Greg's new car, were awful warnings against strange men and extravagance as well as the usual one against falling on one's head.

Lying on a blanket by the stream, with cherry blossom arched against the blue sky and the sunlight yellow of celandines all round me, I tried to compose a calming reply.

I wrote that Mr Melville was old and fussy, that Chris, though helpful and friendly, was not my type, that Mark preferred Lisa and that Trevor, who was going to teach me to drive—in absolute safety round the drives and lanes of the Sterne estate—was hideously ugly and had a mass of girl friends already.

Then I walked to the post office by the west drive and the river path and, before ladening myself with shopping, I explored the village and looked round the church, which was full of Sterne tombs and brasses.

When Lisa came back-she'd been lunching with a cousin in Salisbury-she disappointed me by failing to notice the immaculate state of the cottage.

"Tea?" I offered. "The kettle's hot."

"I don't think I've time. Look at my hair." Turning to the mirror she gave her reflection an angry glance. "Mark's picking me up at seven-thirty and I've five salmon trout to garnish and a cold table to set when I've changed. But this group moves on tomorrow, thank God! Some country house hotel between Oxford and Stratford is their next stop, and the new lot aren't due for two weeks."

"Here." I handed her a mug of tea. "Tourists sound even more demanding than horses."

Later, I was doing evening stables when Lisa, stumbling painfully over the cobblestones in her high heels, gave me an airy wavy and called "Bye, don't wait up." she had put her hair up and was wearing a simple black dress with her Peruvian necklace of beaten silver and long, matching earings.

Suddenly I felt depressed. If I were wittier and more elegant would I have a better time, I wondered? It wasn't only her success with Mark—she seemed to have a whole network of friends to visit. Why didn't I have cousins, sisters, friends scattered all over the place? Why did Mum have so few relations and why had no one in my father's family ever bothered about me?

As I pushed the wheelbarrow to the muckheap, I wondered how Mum really felt about being so relationless: only Aunt Jenny in Scotland and two cousins we never saw. She'd always been light-hearted about it when

I was young,

"Fewer people to quarrel with," she would laugh. Or, "You choose your friends, but you're landed with your family." But that could have been a cover-up, and it must have been lonely and dreary, living on her own with me when I was little. Then it occurred to me that she had doubled the size of her family by marrying Greg and producing Robbie. And mine, I thought bitterly, for a stepfather and a half-brother young enough to be my son, were hardly ideal relations.

I was in Marmaduke's box, hanging his haynet and still feeling sorry for myself, when I heard footsteps and then Chris's voice calling, "Kate?"

"With Marmaduke," I answered.

"Fancy coming out for a pizza?" Chris's head looked over the door. "I suddenly woke up to the fact that it was your day off, but I was too cowardly to phone the Castle, so I came round on the off chance. It's O.K. if you've other plans."

"I'd love a pizza," I told him, "but I'm wearing my worst jeans and I haven't finished the horses."

"There's time to change, well, half an hour," said Chris, looking at his watch. "What do the horses need?"

"Just Fiesta's haynet and feeds."

When we'd fed the horses Chris sat in the sitting room with a coffee and the tin of chocolate brownies, while I changed.

There was no time for dithering and since all my jeans and sweaters were hanging on the clothes line in the orchard, it had to be a dress.

I emerged in record time and Chris was very encouraging.

"First time I've seen you in a dress. You look stunning, even better than in jeans, and that blue suits you."

I tried to be equally encouraging when he began to apologise for his car." I like old cars," I told him, "they have character."

"Well she's not exactly a veteran, just an old banger, but she is reliable and cheap to run and, by avoiding the yearly depreciation on a new one, I can afford to keep Rufus."

We agreed that the Marks and Adrians of this world relied too heavily on their status symbol possessions and I found myself telling him about my rather impoverished, one-parent upbringing. Chris said that he had two parents, but a brother and two sisters, so they hadn't been particularly well off either.

Then we talked about our childhoods and giggled about the awfulness of our school days and I learned that afterwards Chris had gone to Art School and done a course in design. He wasn't very forthcoming about his job, only saying that he worked for a large firm and could design anything as required.

He'd been abroad quite a bit, mostly with student friends, and his holidays seemed full of adventures with broken-down cars, blown away tents, and invariably ended with running out of money.

We talked without pause all through our pizzas and salad, our ice creams and red wine and coffee, and we were still talking as we drove home.

We climbed the yard gate, checked the horses, and then approached the cottage noisily in case Mark and Lisa were there, but there was no sign of them.

Chris refused coffee, brushed aside my thanks for a

lovely evening, and took himself off, muttering that we might do a movie next Monday.

As I climbed into bed I heared Lisa's key in the lock. She knocked on my door and then peered in.

"Everything all right, no prowlers?"

"I wasn't here. Chris turned up and we went out for a pizza."

"Oh brilliant. I was a bit worried about you, here on your own. Did you have fun? Chris is a bit of an unknown quantity as far as I'm concerned."

"Yes, it was fine. He's very easy to talk to. What was your evening like?" I still had a struggle to keep the resentment out of my voice.

"We had a great time, though the restaurant was a bit disappointing. The *crêpes* were ghastly, really stodgy, and I have done better *moules* myself."

"What did you talk about?"

"Oh food and wine. And a place near San Moritz we both know. Mediterranean holidays, you know, just chat."

I fell asleep still hurt that Mark preferred Lisa, but admitting to myself that it was really more fun to go out with Chris. I felt that he liked the basic, imperfect Kate; with him there was no need to put on an act.

The wonderful spring weather broke in the early hours of Tuesday morning and the rain poured down in monsoon-like torrents instead of the expected April showers. With the paddock waterlogged, schooling was out of the question.

I found my mackintosh and gloves and decided that, as riding one and leading one would mean roadwork, which I hate, I would take each horse for a shorter, and brisker than usual hack.

I was just setting out on Fiesta, when to my surprise the Sternes appeared. They shouted that I was to wait as they were coming with me. I looked at the shapeless figures dressed in an extraordinary assortment of ill-fitting capes and anoraks, and shouted back: "Not without string gloves," for I knew bare, cold hands on slippery reins would lead to unmanageable ponies and give Tarka an opportunity for bolting off.

"Sorry, we haven't got any. We've all lost at least one and Mum won't buy us any more," answered Charlie.

"Oh don't be so fussy, Kate. Delia never made us," argued Felicity.

"Delia didn't make you ride properly or sort out Tarka," I snapped back.

'Don't worry we'll find some. There are lots of odd ones lying around," Ben assured me soothingly.

"But supposing they're the wrong hand?"

"No problem provided they're at least two sizes too big," Charlie explained. "We'll be back."

"In about three-quarters of an hour," I told them as Fiesta, resenting the rain, began to dance and twirl. "And can someone open the park gate, please."

I rode very briskly and when I returned feeling cheerful and invigorated on a steaming Fiesta, I found the Sternes in a high state of excitment.

"Ben's found the keys," Felicity shrieked from the gate.

"It's my story, I want to tell Kate," Ben was protesting.

"Well why don't you get on with it then?" she demanded.

"They were in the china bowl on the table opposite the dining room door," gabbled Ben. "I was looking for lost gloves in the drawers and I suddenly saw them."

"Had they been there all the time?" I asked as I led Fiesta into her box.

"No," they all answered at once. "Everyone had looked there."

"It's the sort place where people do put keys so Mum and Dad are both positive they checked it."

"It means that whoever took them, brought them back, but they probably had copies made first," said Charlie darkly.

"But why bring them back and why put them there?" I asked.

"Because the thief meant to put them back on the board, but someone came out of the dining room, or along the kitchen passage, and he had to dump them quickly," Felicity answered impatiently.

"And it could have been someone who didn't know we'd discovered they were missing," added Charlie. "Only a few people have been told they were lost."

"Lisa thinks that one of the Japanese might have found them and been too embarrassed to say so—she says they're like that." Ben sounded as though he was clutching at straws.

"Who had the opportunity to put them back?" I asked as I rubbed Fiesta dry.

"Dozens of people," answered Felicity. "There were not as many there last Sunday as the one before, but there were still a lot."

"Did anyone pay two visits, I mean one each weekend?" I wondered.

"We could ask the Whites," suggested Felicity. "Amy was selling the tickets both weekends, she might have noticed."

"And I'd better check my notebook," said Ben. "I didn't get all the car numbers the first Sunday, because of being a page, but I think I got most of them last time."

"Doesn't this rule out Mr Melville?" I asked. "He's in and out of the Castle so much, that if someone disturbed him, he could easily have waited for another opportunity to put them back on the key board. I think he would have pocketed them rather than dump them in the bowl. Anyway he must have heard you all talking about them being lost."

"No, I don't think he did. He came up at that practice when I was telling you about the search, but I stopped at once," said Charlie thoughtfully.

On Wednesday it poured again and it was obvious that the jousting practice would have to be cancelled, but Mr Melville spent half the afternoon standing in the tack-room doorway and gazing despondently at the still rain-heavy sky. I found having to say "Excuse me," and push past him every time I went in or out very irritating.

Thursday was ghastly too. The rain bucketed down and the humidity was making everyone edgy. I felt as though I was living at the bottom of a pond and I had run out of dry clothes. Our one-bar electric fire was surrounded by sweaters, jeans and jodhpurs in varying degress of wetness. Lisa complained that the whole cottage smelled of damp horse, and I was reduced to using the hair dryer on the soggy lining of my mac.

Then, with equal suddenness, the rain stopped and the

sun blazed down with summer warmth. The grass, emerging from pools of water, had grown six inches, the trees, reappearing from the mist, were in full leaf.

I hung all my clothes on the line in the orchard and refused to let the Sternes school until the paddock had dried out. I took them for yet another hack, but now, unencumbered by mackintoshes, we were able to practise cross-country riding on the heath.

A hastily arranged jousting practice was rather a disaster. I had exercised the horses every day during the rain, but as there had been no practising or schooling, they were all short of work. Marmaduke, definitely overfresh, was charging about, skidding on the sodden ground and infuriating Mr Melville. Mark seemed on a short fuse too and lost his temper with Trevor, who would chatter about his caparisons and joke when things went wrong.

Everyone seemed off form. When they missed the quintains they blamed me or Charlie for not holding them straight. Rings, pursued by curses, were flying all over the lists and no one seemed able to carry a head for four lengths.

But by the time we got to the jousting the horses had settled down and Chris began well with a strike on Trevor and then another on Mr Melville. Mark also scored on Trevor and then he and Chris had a double strike, which cheered everyone up.

In the final ride, Mark against Mr Melville, something went wrong. Mark said afterwards that the overfresh Marmaduke had swerved at the last minute, but whatever the cause, he struck Mr Melville bang in the middle of his shield, very nearly unhorsing him, and then dropping his lance, he clutched his wrist and swore loudly.

Mr Melville, who had also dropped his lance, was stir-rupless and swaying in his saddle, but managed to pull up safely.

We all hurried to Mark, who was still clutching his wrist, and we were offering first aid when a red-faced and spluttering Mr Melville trotted over.

"What the hell were you playing at, Mark? You know that if you're not in a good position you don't attempt a strike; it's the first rule of the game. You nearly had me off, you could have given me a really nasty fall."

"Yes, I know and I'm sorry," answered Mark as his face twisted with pain.

"I think it's broken, I'll fetch my car and drive you to Oddstock Hospital for an x-ray," said Chris.

"No, no, I guess it's only a sprain. Look, I can move my fingers."

"Can you grip my hand?" asked Chris.

"Half a minute, don't panic, I've got my first-aid kit." called Trevor running towards us from the Land Rover.

"No thank you, finger bandages and plasters aren't required," said Mark scornfully. "I'll get it strapped up one the way home."

"But it's a good kit," Trevor protested "I got it at the AA shop and I know there's a sling in it."

"There are some elasticated bandages in the tackroom cupboard, I could strap you up now," I suggested.

"No thank you." Mark's voice was irritable with pain. "All I need is a lift to my car."

Charlie and I hastily loaded the lances and other gear into the Land Rover while Chris and Trevor helped Mark to dismount and installed him in the passenger seat.

"I'll let you have a progress report tomorrow, Walter," he called as Trevor drove him away, but Mr Melville, still red-faced and fuming, only glared.

"Got your hat?" I asked Charlie. "Good, you have Fiesta then; time you rode a well-schooled horse."

We rode home sadly and Mr Melville, his anger abating, began to lament the loss of our best man and the devasting defeat in the grand tournament that now faced us.

"He insists that he's O.K. to drive," said a worried-looking Trevor as we watched Mark's BMW cruising down the drive. "Lucky it's an automatic because he seemed in a lot of pain. Can you give us a hand unloading this lot, Charlie?"

The practice had ended late and everyone was in a rush to get away. I unsaddled Fiesta, helped Trevor hitch up his trailer and hurried Charlie off to his dinner.

"I've got to go too," Chris told me, "But *please* be sensible, Kate. The dirty saddlemarks and the tack cleaning can wait. All the horses are going to be out again tomorrow, and then we'll do one of your Kingsdown clean-ups for Sunday."

"It's the laying the table deadline that counts," I told him.

"Even my Kingsdown training can't stand up to Lisa's glares. I won't have time to do more than water and lock up."

"You're still worrying about the prowlers then?" asked Chris, dumping his tack.

"Yes, especially at weekends, that's when they came before."

It was true that we were still worried, despite the padlocks, and for some reason both Lisa and I were very jumpy that night. She said she knew she wouldn't be able to sleep, so she was going to sit up and listen for 'them' and I tried to keep her company. But, though I drank several cups of black coffee, I kept falling asleep in the chair, until Lisa, tired of my lack of conversation, said: "Oh for heaven's sake go to bed. I'll wake you if rape looks imminent or they start stealing the horses."

On Saturday morning everyone except Mark appeared early. Trevor was first, with Fixit fully caparisoned.

Called to inspect, I had to admit that the black and gold horsecloth was really spectacular and that it made Fixit look huge, and very formidable. Trevor was impressive too. Dressed entirely in black, except for the gilded crest and plume of his helm and the gold cross on his shield, he looked dramatically sinister. I considered asking what had made him abandon the fesse vert, about which we'd heard so much, but decided I hadn't time to listen to the answer.

As I flew around, brushing out saddlemarks and removing straw from manes, Trevor sat on Fixit, and was photographed by the usual gang of family and friends. Then Chris appeared and took him off to the lists. Mr Melville, who announced that he was going to settle Marmaduke down with a really long hack, also disappeared into the park and the Sternes followed me about, explaining that they wanted to school early because an aunt had come to stay.

"She's our useful aunt," Felicity told me, "and she's offered to go through all the old curtains in the attic with us and make our saddle cloths for tomorrow."

"She says they have to be *hemmed*," complained Ben. "But luckily she's better at sewing than Mum."

"She's flying to Jersey tomorrow, so she's got to get going this morning—that's why we want to ride now," added Charlie.

With all the preparations for the grand tournament crowding upon us we couldn't really concentrate on schooling, so I stopped earlier than usual and organized a handy pony competition. It began with opening the yard gate into the paddock and included jumps, a slip rail and the garden path. I timed everyone and Ben kept the scores in one of his notebooks. Charlie won, because Ben ran out at the grid and Felicity lost time at the gate.

When we went in we found that Mr Melville was already back from his ride and he explained that he had to meet some of the Lyme people to discuss final arrangements. Then, as I brushed over Fiesta, he insisted on telling me where the two loo tents, the drinks' stall and the two little pavilion tents were all to be sited.

When he drew breath I asked if there was any news of Mark.

"It doesn't sound too good," he answered gloomily. "He's had it strapped up and he says the medical advice is, "We'd rather you didn't, but if you must you can". So he'll be here, though I can't see a chance of him being on top form. He wants me to give him a rest during the heads and the rings, but that won't please the Lyme people, I'd more or less promised them we'd field four in everything this time. Anyway we've agreed to postpone the final decision until the morning. It's too bad that this had to happen now," he went on in a querulous voice. "Our first big event and coachloads of tourists coming from France and Holland. Have you seen the adverts?"

"No." I shook my head.

"Oh they're all over the place. The Lyme people have done a great job. One unfortunate thing though—they billed the tournament as 'taking place in the presence of Lord Sterne'. I don't know where they got that idea from, it seems they thought it would bring more people in and they say that Mark encouraged them. Of course people do love a Lord, especially foreigners. But I've had a terrible time persuading his Lordship. He's become such a recluse, you see. Hardly goes out and spends all his time shut up with that coin collection of his; it can't be healthy."

"No, it certainly can't," I agreed quickly, "and I think Mrs Sterne is afraid that Charlie will go the same way. Look, I must get on. I'm going to take Fiesta out for at least two hours as the last thing Mark will want is an overfresh horse."

TEN

Sunday began with a shower, but by the time the advance party from Lyme had arrived with the tents, it was a glorious day with the fresh, green countryside smelling of trees and flowers and wet, warm earth.

The Sternes, having demanded buckets of warm water from the cottage and the loan of Fiesta's shampoo, set to work briskly. When I had finished drying Fiesta, I was called to inspect a dripping Romany and meanly pointed out that she had grass-stained hocks, and dried mud behind her ears and on her chest.

"I'm really glad that I've got an absolutely plain pony, "said Charlie as he dragged me off for his inspection. "Tarka's brilliant to groom, not the smallest white sock and a nice easy mane."

"Two burrs in his tail," I observed, running my hand over the pony, 'but otherwise he's fine."

As soon as I passed Snowy and Romany fit for processions, Felicity and Ben rushed off to see what the Lyme people were doing, but Charlie stayed, following me round and talking ceaselessly until I put him to work,

166

grooming the lower sections of Marmaduke and Rufus, while I dealt with the elevated ones. Then I invited him to share my coffee break and as we drank coffee and ate chocolate brownies, we discussed school.

"It's mostly boring and not many people like me," he confided gloomily. "Of course I'm no good at any sport and I really hate football. I've only got two friends, David and Mike. They're both computer buffs like me."

"But two friends sounds quite normal," I objected. "I only had two, well two who lasted, and I never felt hard done by."

"But Felicity and Ben have dozens," he argued. "On their birthdays they always want to ask at least twenty people and I only want two."

"Parties are different," I told him. "You ask acquaintances and people whom you think you might like, not just real friends. And as for sport you're becoming quite a respectable rider, so stop moaning."

Cheered by my praise, Charlie became energetic and oiled all twenty-four hoofs, while I finished Rufus. Then helped me fill the evening haynets and take round the lunchtime feeds.

By the time Chris arrived, confessing guiltily to having overslept, I was heading for the cottage and planning a quiet lunch before I changed into my fancy dress. I told him that everything was ready, and suggested that he left the horses to digest their feeds in peace and went to see what the Lyme people had been doing.

Mark was late, and Mr Melville, in an acute state of fuss, became convinced that the wrist was worse and that he wouldn't turn up. But, just as Trevor and the Sternes returned from delivering the gear to the lists and Chris and I had caparisoned and tacked up Fiesta, Mark strolled in. He answered all our anxious inquiries with a wave of the strapped up wrist and, without a word to anyone, disappeared into the spare loosebox to change.

"Oh dear, oh dear," fussed Mr Melville. "That doesn't look too good. I think he must be in pain. Do you think you should see if he wants any help with changing, Chris?"

"No, I took that silent wave to mean 'shut up and leave me alone'," Chris answered. "He'll call if he wants us."

Despite two minor panics—first Charlie couldn't slide the tabs of the useful aunt's rein decoration over the buckle of his rein and then Felicity noticed that Ben was riding with a twisted girth—the Knights of Sterne and their pages were ready on time. As I handed out banners and pennants I saw that someone, probably the useful aunt, had provided Ben with a baldric. It was a sort of diagonal belt, from one shoulder to the opposite hip, and his bugle was attached to it, leaving him with both hands free. Charlie was wearing a red sash, also tied baldric-fashion, which made him look much less solid.

As the only Sterne walker left I opted out of the procession I didn't want to march with the Lyme people and, anyway, they all had their pairs, so I told Mr Melville that I would sneak up ahead and take the ponies' headcollars. This meant that I was able to join the crowd and watch the procession approach.

It was a wonderful sight. The ponies in their bright saddle cloths, with matching decorations on their reins, looked tremendously proud, and the eight following knights looked absolutely real. Mark, who was paired with Chris, seemed to have Fiesta under control though she was showing off with her usual shamelessness, and behind them the prancing Marmaduke and the stately Fixit, were clearly warhorses of the highest class.

The procession entered the lists to tremendous applause and I watched Tarka anxiously, but though he was looking round with head high and ears pricked, he showed no sign of misbehaving, and Charlie looked quite calm and was talking to him. Ben was obviously enjoying all the attention that Romany was getting from the children, and Snowy, looking wise and noble, had his fans too.

When they were all lined up facing the pavilion, the music stopped and the commentary began. The Lyme commentator, who was obviously much more experienced than Mr Sterne, read out the potted history of the Castle and then started demanding 'big hands' for everyone in turn. He began with Lord Sterne who I suddenly realized was in the pavilion, looking like an old bald Charlie. He obviously hated his 'big hand' and cowered between the two ladies in medieval dress. There were more 'big hands' for the knights as they galloped their introductionary laps and had their imaginary biographies read out. Trevor had become the noble Sir Tristram Froissard and I found that I could almost believe it as I watch the magnificent figure galloping round.

As we put on the ponies' headcollars and tied them to the spinney railings, Felicity said that she was helping me with the quintains as Charlie had brought his pocket calculator and thought he'd be more use helping the medieval ladies with the scoring.

With so much depending on the state of Mark's wrist, there was great relief in the Sterne camp when he quintained with all his usual skill. Mr Melville was in good form too and Chris gave his best performance ever. When Trevor scored twice our hopes shot up and Ben began to talk of winning. But then disaster struck. As we were putting the quintains away and getting out the rings, we found a long-faced Mr Melville, calling urgently for Chris and Trevor.

"Would you believe it, Mark's not feeling too good," he told them. "He's now gone down with a *tummy bug*. I don't know, it's one dam' thing after another."

"I don't think there's anything in my first-aid kit," began Trevor.

"No, no. He's got some stuff he took on his holiday and he says he's already taken a couple of stiff doses and he's gone down to his car for a third."

"Poor old Mark, he is having a rough time. Shall I go down and see if he needs help?" offered Chris.

"No, no, he says he'll be all right and I don't want any more of you wandering off. The problem is that while he's hoping the medicine will work in time for the joust, he says he feels too groggy for the heads and the rings."

"So we have to ask the Lymes if they mind only fielding three again?" said Chris.

"Precisely. And you'd both better come with me because they're not going to like it."

Felicity and I watched the single-stick fighters gloomily and tried to explain to Trevor's supporters, whose feelings had been hurt when a querulous Mr Melville told them to take their cameras elsewhere, that though the Lyme people would agree to withdrawing one knight, it would be their weakest member, while we had lost Mark, our best.

As we started the rings the commentator announced the score: Sterne and Lyme were equal, running neck and neck, but, he added, the noble Sir Marcus de Salis of Sterne was temporarily indisposed and the chivalrous Knights of Lyme had therefore agreed to withdraw one of their knights from the contest.

"We haven't a hope now," said Ben appearing beside me.

"No, it's bad luck," I agreed, "but there'll be other tournaments. Is there any sign of Mark?" I asked, as the yellow knight thundered by.

"No, but Fiesta's tied to the railings behind the 'gents'. Do you want me to go and see?"

"She'll break her reins," I said, seeing further disasters.

"No, she's O.K., he's put a headcollar over her bridle," Ben reassured me, as I hurried forward to re-stock the quintain arm with rings.

During the interval Chris went down to see Mark, and I pursued Tarka, who had slipped his headcollar and was trotting round, saddlecloth askew, frightening unhorsy members of the public. When I cornered him behind the pavilion with the assistance of several knights of Lyme, I called for Charlie, but it was Felicity, spreading heads, who answered,

"He's gone to fetch something from the castle. He took Snowy, because he thought Tarka might bolt off."

Cursing children who didn't keep an eye on their ponies, I led Tarka to his headcollar with my belt round his neck, and, having moved him and Romany along the railings to fresh grass, I raced back to the lance rack to tighten girths and hand out spears.

The knights tore up and down with Chris and Trevor war-whooping as loudly as the Lyme knights and waving triumphal spears each time they collected a grisly head.

"We're not doing too badly." Ben joined me, notebook in hand.

"And Chris spoke to Mark—he's going to be O.K. for the joust."

"Great, but where *has* Charlie got to?" I asked looking round.

"He went home. I expect he saw his computer and forgot all about the joust. He's like that," observed Ben, a slight note of contempt in his voice.

I helped collect up the heads as the Lyme men-at-arms staged their sword fights and the horses had a rest.

"There's no sign of Charlie or Snowy," I told Felicity. "No, grandfather seems to be helping with the scoring now; those medieval ladies are hopeless."

Our knights began calling for their helms and lances.

"Isn't Rufus going well? I can't get over it," said Chris as he took his helm. Impossible to believe that only three weeks ago we were writing him off.

"You've improved too," I reminded him.

"Where *is* Mark?" fussed Mr Melville.

"Don't panic, he's on his way." Trevor pointed, and we saw Mark and Fiesta coming up the park at a collected canter. Mark was already helmed. I fetched his lance and shield.

"Are you all right, Mark?" Mr Melville fussed round him.

"Yes, I'll be fine. I'm high on whatever they put in these remedies, morphine, I guess."

The commentator, who had said his piece on the history and dangers of mounted combat, began to call for that grand old knight Sir Walter Melville to come and open the joust.

"Not so much of the old," muttered Mr Melville testily as he rode into the lists.

"Don't forget to bridle the ponies for the final procession," I reminded Felicity and Ben. "And if you see Charlie remind him."

Mr Melville began with a perfect strike, but Mark, for whom the commentator demanded a big hand, as he was riding despite his indisposition, missed. However Chris, who suddenly seemed to have developed a killer instinct, gave his opponent a hefty blow, and when Trevor actually scored, against the younger red knight, there were tremendous cheers from the Sterne end.

I was too busy taking helm, shield and lance from the returning knight and dispatching the next one with shouts of 'good luck', to keep the scores and winning seemed unlikely with Mark missing in two events. But, as the last knight rode out and I exchanged the lance for a pennent, I was filled with a quiet, swelling pride that my horses had gone so well and looked so lovely.

"What are we to do—we can't find Charlie or Snowy. I've no one to ride with," complained Felicity.

"You'd better ride with Ben, I'll give him Charlie's banner," I told her. As I fetched the banner the final score was announced. Lyme had won again, but only by three points.

"Well done, Team," said Mr Melville. "Considering the problems it was a first-class show."

"This was the man of the match," announced Trevor,

thumping Chris on the back.

"No, it was Mark, riding despite his afflictions," Chris answered. "Without his score we'd have been way down."

"And with his normal score we'd have won," said Mr Melville, watching the Lyme knights make their lap of honour. "Pages, you'd better lead the way for the victors. The vanquished will follow behind."

"I don't feel vanquished," observed Chris with his wry grin.

Half way down the park the knights broke rank and Lyme and Sterne rode together in gossiping groups. I had left Trevor's supporters to load the Land Rover and hurried down to the yard. I was worrying about Charlie. Supposing he had fallen off and was lying somewhere with a broken leg? To my relief I saw that Snowy, still tacked up, was standing in his box.

"Charlie," I called, trying the loose box first. There was no sign of him. Whipping off the saddle and bridle I made for the tackroom. No sign and no note. I'd left the cottage locked, so I ran round the other boxes, looking over the doors and calling "Charlie!" Absolutely no sign of him.

I ran to meet Felicity and Ben at the yard gate.

"Snowy's here—he was still tacked up, but no sign of Charlie. I'm getting worried."

"Perhaps he's caught Mark's bug." Felicity giggled.

"He might be in the 'gents'," agreed Ben.

"O.K., you ride over and check."

Mark was coming out of Fiesta's box with an armful of caparisons.

"Can you take over, Kate?" he asked. "I'm feeling

ghastly. Absolutely all in. I'll go straight home to bed."

He did look ill, his face was white and drained.

"Would you like some tea, or I could try the Sternes for brandy?" I suggested, as he handed me the caparisons. He shook his head. "Shouldn't you wait and let Chris drive you home?" I called to his back as he hurried out of the yard. But he didn't answer.

Then Felicity and Ben returned, squeezing their ponies through the jam of departing cars.

"He's not there."

"You're sure."

"Positive. I held Rom and Ben went in."

"What can have happened? We haven't seen him for ages. Do you know what this errand was?" I asked.

"Ben knows."

"It was for one of the men-at-arms. He came into the pavilion and said he couldn't fight because the strap on his leg armour had broken and he was wearing red and yellow tartan socks. Then Charlie remembered the armour we found in the armoury the other day when we were looking for the keys. It wasn't real, Mum thought Great-Grandfather or someone had it made for a party. Charlie said he was sure there were leg pieces and he'd ride down and fetch them."

"We'd better go home and look for him," said Felicity. "He may have started messing about with his computer and forgotten the jousting."

"Yes. Well bundle the ponies into the field, I'll feed them. And, if you don't come back, I'll know you've found him," I told her, as Mr Melville rode into the yard.

"Can you take him, Kate?" he asked, dismounting

stiffly and handing me Marmaduke's reins. "Frank Grigson wants a quick word about next time and you can't move out there, it's like Piccadilly Circus." He hurried away before I had time to tell him about Mark or the missing Charlie.

I told Chris as we rushed round topping up buckets and brushing out sadddlemarks.

"I'm sorry about Mark driving home like that," Chris shouted to be heard above the running tap, "but he's not the easiest person to help. As for Charlie, I expect a friend turned up and took him off to play football, or whatever game kids in castles play."

Felicity and Ben didn't reappear. We fed the horses and ponies and Chris began to talk about a tea-break before tack cleaning, but I was still anxious.

"It's out of character," I explained. "The others might have wandered off with friends, but not Charlie; he's got a 'one thing at a time' brain and he's conscientious."

"Kate, there's no sense in worrying." Chris tried to sound masterful. "We'll go over to the Castle now, this minute, and make quite sure they've found him. Then we'll be able to have our tea in peace. Come on, if all is well, we may even get a free tour."

The main rush of cars from the park into the drive had reduced to a trickle. All the Lyme transport had gone and the only car left outside the garages belonged to Chris. A few of the spectators were still picnicking or strolling about the park enjoying the sunshine and listening to the wood pigeons, who had begun their evening coo. After the hectic day, it all seemed very peaceful. But then, as we crossed the drawbridge, we saw Felicity and Ben burst from the Castle porch. They were running in our direction and, when they caught sight of us, they waved and shouted.

"Looks like bad news," said Chris as we ran to meet them. They were both out of breath and crying.

"What's happened?" I asked.

"Charlie's gone," cried Ben.

"Grandfather's coin collection has been stolen!" Felicity was gulping to control her tears, "and Charlie's vanished. We've found his specs, smashed on the armoury floor. We think he's been kidnapped."

"He can't see a thing without them," sobbed Ben.

"Do your parents know?"

"Has someone sent for the police?" Chris and I both spoke at once.

"Dad's still at cricket and Mum's taken Aunt Carola to the airport. Grandfather says he's rung the police but only about the coins, he doesn't believe that Charlie's been kidnapped. He says he must be around somewhere. But he's not. We've searched everywhere."

Kidnapping seemed a bit unlikely to me too. I glanced at Chris. "We'd better take a look."

Chris nodded.

"Yes, come on." Felicity set off at a run.

"They'll be miles away by now," sobbed Ben, stumbling along behind.

Chris reached the Castle first, but waited for Felicity to fling open the oak door and lead us into the great hall. We turned left down what I knew to be the dining room passage and then right. We burst through a door covered in green baize. The passage was stone-flagged now and clattered under our feet, and baking smells told me that we were passing the kitchens. We came to another door, ancient, iron-bound with a small barred window. It creaked and groaned as Felicity and Chris tugged it open. A sudden chill of cold damp air met us as we plunged down a narrow flight of stone steps into dungeon gloom, for there were only a few slits in the thick walls and a low, knee-high arch, to let in the light.

Felicity fumbled for a light switch and then a single, shadeless bulb showed us a room that was round, its rough stone walls hung with ancient weapons, its uneven floor strewn with old cannon, stone cannon balls, sagging chests and rusted junk.

"Look, there," Felicity pointed. The glasses lay crushed, as though trodden on, twisted wire rims and broken lenses.

"They're Charlie's."

"You're sure?" Chris squatted for a better look. "You're certain that they're not an old pair that he could have lost down here some time ago?"

"Certain. They were new and he hated them. He thought they made him look like Piggy in *Lord of the Flies*, but he had to have them; the ones he wanted were too expensive."

I picked my way through the chests and cannon balls to the arch. It opened on the moat, the only stretch of moat that was still full of water. I crouched and saw that a small flight of stone steps led down into the stream and the heavy iron grating which should have protected the arch was open; four bars had been sawn through and whatever had locked the two sections together had vanished. Probably it lay on the floor of the stream.

"This is where they broke in," I said.

"They could have got the coins out that way too,"

observed Chris.

"And Charlie," added Ben tearfully.

"We"d better get out of here, we're trampling on clues," Chris went on. "Do you think you should have a word with Lord Sterne? The police take their time about coming to burglaries, but if Charlie's really missing they ought to get their skates on."

"Yes, please do, Kate. He might believe you."

"Where is he?"

We all followed Felicity up a spiral stone staircase. It seemed to be in a turret and was so narrow that my arms brushed against both walls at once. We climbed and climbed until giddy and breathless, we suddenly emerged into a brightly-lit room full of glass showcases. Sitting on a chair and gazing blankly at his empty cases was Lord Sterne.

He seemed stunned and hardly aware of our unceremonious arrival.

"Lord Sterne," I spoke loudly, hoping to bring him back to life. "We think you ought to telephone the police again and tell them that Charlie's missing." His dazed eyes gazed at me vaguely. "The thieves broke into the armoury from the stream," I went on, "Charlie was there, fetching some armour. We think he saw the thieves and they've kidnapped him, taken him hostage. His broken spectacles are lying on the floor of the armoury and we can't find him. Mr and Mrs Sterne are both out," I added, "so it has to be you."

"Would you like me to do it?" offered Chris.

"It's really urgent," I was almost shouting. "They may kill Charlie if you don't get the police at once." I knew I would upset Ben and Felicity, but I had to rouse Lord

Sterne somehow, and as they both burst into noisy tears, he got to his feet.

"Charlie's missing?" he said. "You think he may have seen the thieves?" He picked up the telephone and dialled slowly.

"The two keys that went missing were the armoury and the west gate," I muttered at Chris.

"Yes, but they've had hours to get away," he answered.

"We can't be sure. They may have found Charlie when they came *in*." I stopped, Lord Sterne was talking to the police.

"Yes that's right, a burglary and now my grandson is missing. There's a possibility that he may have surprised the thieves. He's ten, no, eleven. Yes, he came back to the castle alone." He looked to us for confirmation. "Yes, we were all watching the jousting. Yes, and his spectacles have been found, broken. In the armoury, yes that seems to be where they broke in." He put down the receiver slowly. "They're on their way. Someone had better find White." He looked at Felicity. "What time is your mother expected back?"

"I'm not sure."

"Will you and Ben find Mr White and tell him what's happened," I asked Felicity. "Chris and I are going to check the west gate.

"If the police want us we'll be checking the west gate," I repeated to Lord Sterne. "You remember that its key also went missing."

"Yes, yes, I'll tell the police about the keys." He got up.

"Meanwhile I had better start looking for Charlie."

We didn't tell him that the Castle had been searched.

Any activity seemed better than staring at empty glass
cases. We followed Felicity, who led us out of the
armoury tower and along a passage to the main staircase.

Filled with foreboding and appalled by the amount of
time already wasted, I ran down the wide staircase,
through the Great Hall, and out across the lawn. Chris
passed me and raced ahead, shouting that we'd take the
car. By the time I reached the garages he had the engine
running and the passenger door open. As I banged it
shut we shot into the drive. Then Chris, preparing to
turn into west drive, began to curse. There was a large
tourist coach, blocking the entrance. There were no
passengers on board, but a relaxed looking driver was
reading, his newspaper spread over the steering wheel.

"Hi, can you let us through?" Chris called. "We've got
to get down to the stream; it's an emergency."

"Sorry mate. Can't help, she's broken down. We
pushed her here to clear the main drive. The company
sent a relief coach and now I'm waiting for the break-
down truck."

"Through the paddock," I said, checking that the keys
to the gates were still on the chain round my neck.

"What's going on?" called the coach driver as Chris
reversed wildly, causing the driver of a homebound
family to hoot indignantly, "You're the second bloke
trying to get down here in a tearing hurry."

"The *second* bloke," I thought as I tugged open the
stable gate and ran across the yard to the paddock one. It
sounded as though we might be on the right track. I
flung myself back into the car for the bumpy ride
across the paddock and out again at the far gate. I tried to
be calm, but I couldn't stop my shaking hands fumbling

with the key.

Then we were in the west drive, as the car lurched from pothole to pothole, we looked ahead to the bridge. My heart sank, we were too late. There were no cars or people to be seen.

"We'd better check the bridge. If they used a boat they may have abandoned it here," said Chris, turning on to the river path and stopping. We stood on the bridge. I shaded my eyes from the setting sun and gazed up the long drive. It was deserted and the gate at the far end was shut. Chris was hanging over the parapet trying to see if anything was concealed below. We went down and searched among the arches and roughly-built stone piers. I took off my boots and cursed my tight velvet trousers, as I waded in for a closer look. The water was rising, which meant that the mill pool sluice had been closed, but there was nothing, no boat, no hidden packages, no Charlie.

We stood on the bridge again, looking upstream to the Castle. All was peaceful, the only sound the coo of the wood pigeons, the only movement a pair of mallard ducks drifting gently downstream.

"We'd better check the gate," said Chris despondently.

"We've forgotten the boathouse," I cried, appalled at our stupidity, but, now that the trees were in full leaf, it was almost hidden. We both ran along the path and I launched myself on to the nearest of the narrow landing stages which edged the channel of water leading to the double doors.

"Careful!" Chris grabbed my arm as the rotten wood sagged and sank beneath my weight. "I don't think anyone could have got in that way," he added as he pulled me back to land. "Is there another door?"

Forcing our way through a jungle of thorn bushes, sycamore saplings and brambles, we found the other door. It was for people rather than boats, and a new-looking hasp and padlock, barred our entry.

Chris rattled the door and swore.

"It's too new for a Sterne padlock," I told him and, braving the thorn bushes, I made for a loose plank in the boathouse wall. Prising it outwards, I peered in. My eyes gradually adapted to the dim light provided by a broken skylight. A narrow slatted landing stage ran round three sides of the boathouse and, in the centre, bobbing gently on the murky water, was an inflatable dinghy.

"There's a boat in there, a rubber dinghy," I called to Chris. He crashed through the bushes. I made room for him at my peephole.

"It looks newish," I told him. "Too new to belong to the Sternes."

"Are you sure?"

"Yes, and the children told me that the boathouse wasn't used any more."

"I'd better break down the door then."

We fought our way out of the bushes and Chris flung himself against the door. When his weight failed to move it he began kicking the handle.

As I stood waiting, my feeling of foreboding returned.

"Perhaps I could get on the roof and drop through the broken skylight," I suggested.

"No, you'll kill yourself." Chris stopped using brute force and was examining the hasp. "This is new, but the wood they've screwed it into is pretty rotten. If I had something strong I could lever it off."

We both looked round. There were bits of wood lying everywhere, but they were as rotten as the door.

"Car tools," said Chris suddenly, and raced away, crashing through the bushes, as he made for the river path.

While he was gone, I kicked and banged and threw my weight against the door without the least effect, but it felt better than simply waiting.

"Tyre lever, this should do it," said Chris, dropping a tool kit at my feet. With a couple of heaves the hasp began to bend and give way, then the screws began to loosen in the wood. Chris heaved again. The screws pattered on to the leaves and the door swung open.

We went in cautiously, and turning opposite ways, we crept gingerly along the slatted landing stages. Chris had made for the boat's painter, which was tied to an iron ring. He began to pull the rubber dinghy in for a closer look. I crept on towards the double doors. There was a new padlock on them too. They were locked on the *inside*. Someone was using the boathouse, but there was no coin collection hidden there, no Charlie.

I was about to tell Chris that we should waste no more time, but go back and tell the police what we knew, when the feel of the landing stage, which had been dipping and sinking under each step I took, suddenly changed. It became solid as though supported from below. I crouched down and felt the slimy slats with my hands. There was some rough cloth beneath the slats. I felt again. Some of it was dry. There wasn't enough light to see properly, but it seemed like one of those heavy old-fashioned sacks in which the home farm still sent our chaff and it was full.

Suddenly I was frightened. "Chris," I called in a quavering voice, "There's something here."

"What sort of thing?"

"A sack with something in it, jammed under the landing stage."

"We need a light. Hang on a sec, I've got a torch with the tools."

The landing stages rocked and squelched as he made for the door. My fear of what was inside the sack was growing. It didn't feel hard enough for the cases that held the coins. Kneeling on the slats I plunged my arms deep in the stagnant water and began to tug at the thick sackcloth. I had to get it out. I pulled frantically, but I couldn't move it. My own weight on the landing stage was holding it down. I moved back.

"We'll have to use the dinghy to pull it out. We must be quick," I said as Chris shone the torch.

"You're right, it is a sack and it hasn't been there long." There was a note of dread in his voice too. "I'm going in," he added, "It can't be deep, but there's probably a lot of mud,"

I took the torch as he slid into the water. It reached over his knees.

"Practically solid mud," he said moving along the landing stage with slow, squelching steps. Then he began to ease the sack out from under the landing stage. He handed the securely tied mouth of the sack to me.

"Here, this part's still dry. For God's sake keep it out of the water. Now, move along a bit and I'll heave the rest up."

Chris heaved and I pulled, and the rest of the muddy, waterlogged sack came up out of the water. We eased it along the landing stage to the door. As Chris struggled free of the mud I felt in my anorak pockets for my knife.

"I think it moved," I said, my voice trembling.

"Let's get it out into the open."

We carried the heavy sack through the bushes and brambles and laid it gently beside the path. As I began to saw through the cord which tied the mouth we heard an engine. I went on sawing, but Chris said, "Police car!" And standing up began to wave and shout, "Over here."

The cord gave and the mouth of the sack opened revealing pale hair.

"Is this the missing boy?" asked a policeman kneeling beside me.

"Yes, that's Charlie," I answered as his body slithered from the wet sack and we saw that his hands were tied with cord and his mouth gagged with his red sash.

Pulling off the gag, one policeman rolled him over, the other took my knife and began to free his hands. We watched desperately, hoping and praying for a sign of life.

"Was he under water, submerged like?" asked the policeman.

"No, not completely," Chris answered. "The boathouse has silted up. The sack was under the landing stage, but resting on about two feet of mud."

"Perhaps they were coming back for him then."

"No, not if they knew anything about the stream," I answered as I realised the full of horror of what had been planned, "When the mill stops work at about five-thirty, they close the sluice gates and the level of the stream rises. He would have been drowned in about another hour."

"He isn't dead, is he?" I asked anxiously. "He's still breathing. Charlie, Charlie?" I tried to rouse him. "We've found you; everything's O.K."

"He's breathing," agreed the policeman, turning Charlie on his side. "But he may have had a bang on the head, his pulse is very slow."

Then Charlie coughed and began to cry.

"My hands, my hands," he moaned as he lay writhing on the grass.

"It's the blood coming back," said the policeman. "Come on, we'll carry him to the car."

We wrapped Charlie in a blanket and while I sat beside him on the back seat, the sergeant explained on the radio that Charlie was found and arranged for an ambulance to meet us at the Castle. The constable went with Chris to the boathouse to see exactly where we had found him. Charlie had stopped crying and begun to shiver. I was talking to him gently, as though he were a frightened pony. "You're all right, Charlie, Kate and Chris are here. It's all O.K. now. In a minute we're going to take you home." And then, as it did seem to calm him, I repeated more or less the same thing all over again.

The constable was left to guard the boathouse and Chris, saying that he would come back for his car later, sat on the other side of Charlie so that he was propped up between us.

The sergeant drove slowly and smoothly, and I rubbed Charlie's hands very gently. The circulation had returned, but he was obviously very confused and asked over and over again what had happened and where he was.

"You're fine now," I told him, "and we're taking you home."

"You're in a car and we're taking you back to your mum," said Chris answering the next query.

"But what happened?" Charlie persisted. "What happened just now?"

I decided on partial truth.

"Some thieves were stealing your grandfather's coin collection," I told him. "We think they took you away. But it's all over now."

Charlie was mercifully silent for a few moments, but then, as we drove over the drawbridge, he said, "I know. I remember now. It was Mark. Mark did it. He was in the armoury and he hit me."

"But Mark was jousting," I reminded him gently. "It was the day of the Grand Tournament and you were a page."

"It *was* Mark," Charlie insisted. "When he saw me he took a musket down from the wall and. . . I don't remember any more." He began to cry and shake and I was very glad to see that Mrs Sterne was waiting at the Castle door.

"And who would this Mark be?" asked the policman, bringing the car smoothly to a halt.

"Mark Chandler, I imagine, one of the knights," answered Chris, in a puzzled voice," but he was up in the park riding in the Tournament all afternoon."

I got out of the car quickly to make room for Mrs Sterne. She took my place saying, "Oh Charlie, darling. What have they done to you?" and she put her arms round him.

"My hands hurt and I'm wet and I've got a headache," Charlie answered. "It was Mark who did it. He was in the armoury and he hit me."

ELEVEN

It was an extraordinary evening. An ambulance took Charlie, still sticking vehemently to his story, off to hospital for x-rays and a general check-up, and Mrs Sterne went with him.

Chris, wearing borrowed trousers and socks, and I and the children were interviewed at first separately and then together by a collection of police, men and women. Others, we were told, had been sent to question Trevor and Mr Melville.

The idea was to compile a minute by minute timetable of the tournament and, though at first I refused to believe that Mark had had time to go anywhere near the Castle, much less steal the coin collection or club Charlie with a musket, by the end of my statement I admitted, with a strange feeling in the pit of my stomach, that it was possible—that he had been absent for quite a time.

Later we were all assembled in the library and a woman inspector took us through the afternoon.

"Now you are all certain that you saw Mark Chandler ride in the first event—the quintain," she said looking through our statements. "You saw him plainly. Agreed?"

We all agreed.

Then he went to his car for medicine. No one saw him after that, but his horse was tied up outside the gentlemen's toilet. In the interval Mr Clarke rode down and talked to him from outside the toilet. "But you didn't see him?" she asked Chris.

"No, I shouted, 'Mark, are you O.K.?' and he answered, 'I'll survive', or something like that."

"Are you sure that it was his voice?" asked the Inspector.

Chris thought deeply. "I remember thinking that he sounded pretty groggy," he answered. "It could have been his voice, I assumed it was, but I couldn't swear to it."

"None of you saw him during the spearing of the heads," the inspector went on, "but you all saw him during the joust. Is that right?" She looked round at our faces. "You are all quite certain that he was there for the joust?"

"Positive," said Felicity. "Aren't we, Ben?"

"Yes," Ben waved his notebook. "I can give you his score." But a terrible sinking feeling of doubt had come over me. I had been telling myself and the police, that it *couldn't* be Mark, that poor Charlie was simply confused by a blow on the head. Now in my mind's eye I saw Mark riding up the park at a collected canter and, though he carried neither shield nor lance, he was already wearing his helm. I looked at Chris.

"Did anyone see him without his helm?"

When it transpired that no one had, we explained to the inspector what a helm was and how completely it hid the wearer's face.

"But would someone else have been able to ride the horse and joust instead of him just like that?" she asked.

"Not just anyone, but someone who had come here and practised on that particular horse might get away with it," I answered, my heart sinking lower and lower.

"Adrian Lewis," said Chris. "You're right. He could have answered me from the 'gents' and ridden in the joust."

By the time we had finished explaining to the inspector who Adrian Lewis was, a general call had gone out for the police to pick up him and Mark, and Ben was offering their car numbers.

"They're in one of my other notebooks," he explained. "They both drive BMWs, Mark's is silver and Adrian's red."

Felicity and I helped Ben search through the pockets of several pairs of grubby jeans and jodhs as well as his anorak, before the right notebook was found and, when he had delivered it to the inspector in triumph, Lisa appeared and announced that there was soup and sandwiches for everyone, the police in the library and the rest of us in the Great Hall.

We were all hungry but no one felt in the mood for conversation. It was all too horrible. We could probably have borne the thought of Charlie being mugged and almost murdered by unknown thieves, but that Mark who was one of us, should have done it seemed unthinkable. Everyone passed everyone else soup and spoons and bread and then we sat at the enormous oak table in small, silent groups.

We had finished the soup and Felicity and Chris were

handing round sandwiches when a policeman came in to tell Mr Sterne he was wanted on the phone. A few minutes later he returned smiling.

"Charlie's been x-rayed and there's no serious damage to the skull," he told us, "but they're keeping him in hospital tonight for observation." He turned to his children. "Mum's going to stay with him and I'm to take in some clothes. You'd better come and tell me what they'll need."

Lord Sterne, who had been brooding in a corner and only muttering, "A bad business, a very bad business," in response to offers of food, suddenly got up and, having eaten a sandwich himself, began to press them on Chris and me and a stray policeman.

Pleased that it was Charlie for whom he had been mourning and not he coin collection, I dared to address him.

"I'm so glad Charlie's going to be all right," I said. "I've grown found of him in the short time I've been here and he's really becoming quite a good rider; he loves jumping."

Lord Sterne looked pleased and smiled a small Charlie-like smile.

"Very glad to hear it," he said slowly. "Very glad. There's no doubt that having interests helps one to get through life."

I felt like saying that surely life should be enjoyed rather than 'got through' but then, to my relief Lisa came to clear the dishes and Chris and I who had been looking at each other and wondering if we could leave some time, both rushed to help her.

When we carried the trays of crockery down the long

passage to the kitchen and loaded and started the new dishwasher, Lisa and I decided that we needed some fresh air and that we would walk with Chris to collect his car.

As we walked Lisa asked about finding Charlie. "I don't understand why he was left in the boathouse. Did Mark think he was dead?"

"No, I think he thought he might be alive," I answered, letting the anger I had been suppressing since we found Charlie burst out. "He had bundled him under the landing stage. He must have known that when the mill stops grinding and the sluice gates are closed the water rises. He must have known that by seven o'clock the water would have risen high enough to drown Charlie and there would no witness to give him away."

"It's inconceivable," said Lisa in a horrified voice, as I wiped away some angry tears. "I can't believe that anyone, let alone a man who seemed, well, so nice, could do that to a child."

"He may not have known about the sluice gates, he may have intended to come back later and free Charlie. Or he may have thought he *had* killed him and that it was a body he was hiding," suggested Chris. "Anyway it wasn't premeditated," he went on. "It was done in panic. There he was, thinking that he'd committed the perfect crime and organised himself a cast-iron alibi and Charlie walks into the armoury. Mark, caught in the act of loading the coin collection into the boat, couldn't see a way of talking himself out of it, so he hit the poor kid on the spur of the moment. If he found that he hadn't killed him, he may not have been able to hit him again in cold blood."

"I suppose the dinghy was moored in the archway and that he had taken the chaff sack from the feed store for carrying the cases of coins," I said, trying to derive some comfort from the thought that Mark had lost his head. "But surely the trip back to the boat house would have given him time to think?"

"Not much," answered Chris. "It was downstream, and he must have been fairly desperate. He had to get back to take over from Adrian; the whole plan depended on split-second timing."

"I can't see how they hoped to do the robbery and all this messing about with boats in such a short time," said Lisa.

"They must have had at least one trial run," suggested Chris.

"You mean *they* were our prowlers and they used our orchard landing stage?" asked Lisa indignantly.

"Looks like it," agreed Chris. "They must have cut through the iron bars on the armoury grating before-hand."

"So Adrian Lewis took his car to the boathouse and paddled the dinghy upstream to our orchard." I said slowly. "Then he could have hidden in the gents' loo, taken over Mark's tabard, helm and Fiesta. Meanwhile Mark took the boat from the orchard, stole the coin collection, getting in through the armoury arch. He took Charlie and the dinghy to the boathouse. Drove back in Adrian's car, ready to take over Fiesta. I'm not surprised he looked so white and ill when I met him in the yard; he gave me her caparisons."

"Meanwhile Adrian had picked up his car and tried to belt off down the west drive to collect everything from the boathouse but was thwarted by the broken-down coach. The driver said I was the second bloke," Chris reminded me.

"You think he was supposed to pick up the boat?" I asked.

"Perhaps the boat and Charlie, who knows. It must have been a nasty moment when he found he couldn't get through and if Mark had told him about Charlie, he would have been in a right panic."

"They seem to have got the coins away."

"Yes, Mark must have loaded them into one of the cars."

Suddenly Lisa gave a wail. "Oh *no!* I've just realized that I'm the prat of the year," she said in a horrified voice. "He said he was fascinated by fourteenth century architecture and persuaded me to show him the armoury tower. Oh God, I can't bear it, the whole thing is my fault, the theft and poor Charlie."

"No it isn't, don't be silly, he conned us all," I told her. "The Sternes, Mr Melville. . . *You* didn't agree to stable his horse or to take him on as a knight."

"No, but I was such a fool! Oh I can't bear it, I even showed him the turret staircase, it's supposed to be secret; that's how he got round the burglar alarm."

I was thinking that I would have been just as big a fool if I had been the one with the information Mark wanted. I remembered, with shame, my delight at being asked out for a drink and my chagrin at being dropped in favour of Lisa. What luck, I thought, that I had known so little about the Castle.

"There's no point agonising about it,' Chris was telling Lisa. "We'll all have to put it down to experience. And his cover was brilliant. I mean anyone can ooze charm, hire BMWs, borrow clothes and watches, but to have Mark's riding ability and to own Fiesta. . ."

Poor Lisa, our usual roles were reversed that evening. For, the more we discussed the robbery, the more she realized how much she'd been used. We worked out that both the stealing and restoring of the keys coincided with Mark's visits to the kitchen and as she remembered his questions about the Castle and the Sterne family habits, which she had answered so readily, she sank into deeper and deeper depression.

"How could I have been such a twit, so naive?" she demanded. "I behaved as if I were born yesterday. I can't bear it!"

"It was his smile," I tried to comfort her. "It's a ghastly thought, but I know I would have told him everything, if I'd had anything worth telling."

"But you *were* born yesterday," answered Lisa, sitting at the kitchen table with her head resting in her hands, "*I'm* supposed to be a woman of the world."

"Tea or coffee?" I asked switching on the kettle and opening the cake tin. "Look, why don't you write it all down, that'll stop it whirling round in your head and you'll have it ready to give to the police tomorrow."

Monday was my day off, but I felt that I couldn't leave Sterne before I had news of Charlie. Then there was Lisa in a state and the possibility that the police might need me, I decided to hang around and see what happened. As I fed the horses, rather later than usual, I wondered what would happen to Fiesta. Did the R.S.P.C.A. look after the horses of people who were sent to prison or were they sold to the highest bidder? People like Mark spread mayhem all around them, I thought, for even if Charlie's skull wasn't fractured he had probably suffered psychological damage. I hoped that he had been unconscious when he was trussed up in the sack and had known nothing of the water, rising inch by inch.

It was horrible, so horrible that I didn't believe any ordinary, normal person could have done such a thing and yet it *had* been done and by Mark. I had never believed in evil as a concept, but now I began to wonder if it wasn't the only explanation for Mark.

While I was having breakfast, Felicity and Ben banged on the cottage door.

"Charlie's coming home today," they shouted joyfully.

"Is he all right?" I asked.

"Yes, but because of the concussion he'll have to keep quiet and stay in bed for a week," Felicity answered. "And there's a message from Chris. He says, in case you've forgotten, you're going to a movie tonight and he's picking you up at six forty-five."

"Oh thanks, I'm glad he rang, I *had* forgotten."

"One more thing," said Felicity. "I know it's your day off, but we need to consult you." She produced a typewritten document from behind her back. "This the schedule of the Pony Club twelve-and-under gymkhana. Mum says she'll pay the entry fees and might even buy us new jodhs, if you think we're good enough."

"Charlie told Mum that he wanted to go in the jumping," added Ben, "and she thinks having something to look forward to might stop him having nightmares."

"But you hate the Pony Club and you're not members," I protested.

"Oh yes we are," Ben shouted triumphantly. "Mum's just discovered that dotty Dad forgot to cancel the banker's order so we've paid a family subscription for the whole of this year.'

"What *do* you think about us entering, Kate?" Felicity was trying to keep me to the point. "There'll be plenty of time to practise, after school and at weekends, and Charlie's bound to be better by then."

They both watched my face as I read the schedule. There were all the usual events: jumping, handy pony, bending, musical sacks, egg and spoon. "It sounds perfect," I told them. "Ben can go in all the under ten classes, you and Charlie in the twelve and under."

"Yes, but are we *good* enough," Felicity persisted.

"Good enough to enter or good enough to win?" I asked. "I don't know what the opposition's like round here."

"I think Mum means good enough not to disgrace ourselves like we did last time," she explained

"No, you won't disgrace yourselves. You can tell your mother that, now you've been tidied up, you all ride quite well for your ages."

"Thanks." Shrieking joyfully they rushed away and I went back to my breakfast. I was on my second cup of coffee when Lisa's head appeared round the door.

"I'm taking the police to see the orchard. They've picked up Mark and Adrian. Mark still had the coins in the boot of his car and Adrian was at Heathrow with a flight booked to Caracas."

"Coffee?" I offered.

"No thanks, we drank gallons while they were taking my statement."

In the afternoon I went shopping, for even the cake tin was empty and I could see it staying that way, with Lisa in her present state.

Everyone in the post office wanted to know about the burglary and I explained that the thieves had taken the coin collection and that Charlie had been hit over the head, but I found I couldn't talk about the rest of it. I couldn't tell them of Mark's treachery or that Charlie nearly died.

I stocked up on the basics and added cans of beans and soup and pears to keep us going until Lisa recovered. Then, laden, I wandered back, planning to relax with a book until evening stables.

I was ready when Chris came, but, as there was time to spare I invited him in for a beer and crisps. He knew about Charlie coming home, Felicity had told him when he rang in the morning and about the arrests, because Walter Melville had telephoned him at work.

"Apparently the Castle is saying 'no comment' and referring the press to Walter, so he's in seventh heaven. And there'll be a police statement on the radio and television tonight and in the morning papers," he told me. "But the really interesting gossip came from one of Mark's old mates who got in touch with Walter.

"Apparently Mark and Adrian Lewis went astray when they were working in the City. They were both planning to make their first million by the time they were thirty and when things didn't move fast enough they got into some very shady inside dealing. Then the market collapsed and they were found out and fired. He thinks that Mark's in deep financial trouble, and that stealing the coin collection offered a way out."

"But Mark always acted as though he was loaded," I protested. "The BMW, designer clothes, upmarket holidays and Fiesta."

"The old mate told Walter that he was owed 'a considerable sum', and he thinks Fiesta belongs to an ex-girlfriend at present working abroad."

"That's good news, I was afraid she might be sent to a sale."

We were still talking about Mark when there was a knock on the door and I opened it warily to find Felicity and Ben.

"Come in and have a quick crisp," I suggested.

"Mum said we weren't to disturb you, but she's written you each a note," said Felicity handing out envelopes.

"How's Charlie?"

"Lying in bed and being treated like a prince, even Grandfather's waiting on him," said Felicity jealously.

"We're not allowed in the room because of making a noise," complained Ben.

"It's really weird about Grandfather," Felicity told us. "We all thought his coin collection was his whole life and he'd die without it, but he seems almost pleased it's gone. He says if he gets it back undamaged he'll sell it and spend the money on the Castle. All the experts and the insurance people are very excited and it seems to be much more valuable than he thought it was."

"He'll change his mind," said Ben, sounding almost as cynical as Charlie.

"Yes, he may," agreed Felicity. "And if the coins are scratched or dented they won't be worth much, but if he did get a huge sum of money it would be great; Mum wouldn't have to worry all the time."

When they left we opened our notes.

"Dinner at the Castle next week," Chris sounded horrified. "'A small thank you to both of you for the quick thinking and prompt action which we all believe saved Charlie's life'. Do we have to go?"

"Yes, and she says it will only be the family."

"I haven't got any clothes. What do you wear for dinner in a Castle?"

"Chainmail of course, and you leave your lance and shield in the porch," I giggled.

"Do be serious."

"We'll ask Lisa, she knows that sort of thing. I've got a black and white dress that might do."

Chris looked at his watch, "Time to go if we're going to have a pizza before the movie."

"Can we stop at the post office," I asked, "I ought to make a quick call to Mum, I didn't think of it this afternoon, but I don't want her panicking when she reads about kidnap and robbery in the paper or hears something about Sterne on the news."

As Chris drove us up the drive, I thought how unbelivable it was that only three weeks had passed since I left home. It felt like years. Years spent in a new world, where I had grown older and, in some ways, into a different person.

I had found out so much about myself. I knew now that I was capable of taking 'sole charge', of making decisions, of sharing a cottage, of dealing with demanding knights and teaching tendentious children. And, in the making of that discovery. I had grown far stronger.

As I walked across to the telephone kiosk I tried to see

myself back with Mum in the pre-Greg days and knew that I no longer belonged there, I had my own aims and ideas to try out now, I had to make my own friends and enemies, and I needed my own patch or space, where I could make my own successes and mistakes. At the same time, I knew that I loved Mum just as much; perhaps even more, now that I could see her as a person and not just as my mother—an extension of myself.

"Hullo Mum, it's Kate. How are things?" I asked, determined to get her news before I shattered her with mine.